BBC

# DOCTOR WHO

BBC CHILDREN'S BOOKS

UK | USA | Canada | Ireland | Australia
India | New Zealand | South Africa

BBC Children's Books are published by Puffin Books,
part of the Penguin Random House group of companies
whose addresses can be found at global.penguinrandomhouse.com

www.penguin.co.uk
www.puffin.co.uk
www.ladybird.co.uk

First published by Puffin Books 2011
This edition first published by Puffin Books 2016

001

Written by Richard Dinnick


Printed in Great Britain by Clays Ltd, St Ives plc

A CIP catalogue record for this book is available from the British Library

ISBN: 978-1-405-92256-2

All correspondence to:
BBC Children's Books
Penguin Random House Children's
80 Strand, London WC2R 0RL

BBC

# DOCTOR WHO UNDERWATER WAR

Richard Dinnick

PUFFIN

# Contents

# Chapter 1

# A Submarine in Space

A long way from Earth there was a planet called Hydron. This alien world was almost completely covered in purple water and hung in space like a big grape. Thin wisps of cloud moved slowly across the sky, and the sea below sparkled as light from the planet's nearby star reflected off the tips of the waves.

Round Hydron flew a very large spaceship. It was black and had three long wings that stood out to either side, and another one at the top. This spaceship's name, the *Cosmic Rover*, was painted on the front of the craft in big silver letters. The lower part of the ship bulged out like a pear – this was where everything the ship needed for its mission was stored. And along with the official cargo, the ship also carried an additional item – one that the crew knew nothing about.

Everyone on board the *Cosmic Rover* was busy. The ship had arrived a few hours ago and most crew members were getting ready to go down to Hydron. In all the hustle and bustle, no one noticed the strange sound that had started to come from the storage room. Two crew members walked right past the storage-room door just as the noise became louder, but they were so focused on their task at hand that they didn't notice it either. If they had, they would have said it sounded like a strong wind rising and falling – or perhaps like a snoring giant.

But it wasn't either of those things.

It was the TARDIS arriving.

As the strange blue box finished appearing in the small storage room, a door on the side opened and a woman looked out. She had fiery orange hair and was wearing a red jumper.

'This looks a bit small to be the Tower of London,' she said.

'Some things don't always look like they should, Amy,' said a voice from inside the TARDIS. The voice belonged to a man who now joined Amy outside. He was dressed in a tweed jacket and wore a bow tie.

He looked at the crates and boxes in the cupboard. 'Ah,' he said.

Amy looked at him and bit her lip. 'No, Doctor, they don't. Do they?'

'Ah,' repeated the Doctor. 'No. No. You're right. This isn't the Tower of London.' He started jumping up and down. 'We aren't even on a planet.' He bent down and touched the floor. 'This is a spaceship. A big one. I wonder if this door is locked?'

The Doctor went to look at the metal storage-room door.

A second man appeared in the doorway of the TARDIS. He had spiky hair and was wearing a green T-shirt with a black puffer jacket over the top. 'Oh,' he said. 'Not the Tower of London, then.'

'No, Rory,' the Doctor said with a frown. 'We know that. You must keep up if you don't want to be left behind.'

Rory looked a bit hurt but knew that the Doctor didn't mean it. He knew the Doctor would never leave him behind. He went to look at the door as well. The Doctor was already shaking his head.

'Locked,' he said.

'Sonic!' said Amy, folding her arms.

The Doctor smiled. He put his hand inside his jacket and pulled out the sonic screwdriver. This was the most useful tool in the universe: among lots of other things, it could boil water and tell you if someone's heart was beating, but it was best at opening locked doors.

The sonic screwdriver looked like a thin torch with a green light at the end. The Doctor pointed it at the door and pressed the ON button. The sonic buzzed and the door clicked open.

'Come on, then! I think we should take a look around,' the Doctor said, and marched out into the corridor beyond.

At the front of the ship was the bridge, where all the *Cosmic Rover*'s systems – computers, engines and navigation – could be found. It was a square room with two navigation screens, which showed what was happening outside the ship, taking up most of one side. Against the other walls were computer terminals and the ship's controls. All of the people wore overalls, and each section of the crew had different-coloured overalls: blue for the main crew, black for security and white for medical and scientific.

The ship's captain, Jane Clancy, sat in the command chair. She wore navy-blue overalls with four gold stripes on the sleeves that told everyone her rank. Her soft brown eyes watched the other people on the bridge carefully, and she ran a hand through her curly black hair. Then she put on her captain's baseball cap, in an attempt to keep her hair tidy.

Around her, several crew members were seated in front of computer screens, making final changes to the controls. They had to fly the ship into an exact position above the watery planet. Everyone was concentrating intently on their work, so they didn't notice three new people entering the room.

'Hello,' said the Doctor with a lopsided grin.

Everyone stopped what they were doing and looked up.

'Who are you?' the captain demanded, rising from her chair. 'What are you doing on my ship?'

A man with very pale skin and wearing black overalls stood up. He took a gun from a holster on his belt. 'Stay where you are!' he said.

'It's all right,' the Doctor said. 'I'm the Doctor. This is Amy and Rory.'

Clancy looked at them. 'You can't be pirates,' she said.

'No. Not pirates,' Amy agreed.

'How did you get on board?' asked the man in black.

The Doctor walked up to him and read the name printed on his overalls.

'Mr Fleming? Excellent. Good question, Mr Fleming. You are head of security, I take it?'

'Correct,' said Fleming.

'Good,' said the Doctor. 'Always alert, looking for danger. But we're not dangerous. So you can put the gun away, please.'

The captain nodded and Fleming lowered his weapon.

The Doctor smiled at him and said, 'Thank you.'

'You still need to answer my question,' said the captain. 'How did you get aboard?'

'Ah. Long-range matter transmitter. We beamed in straight from Head Office,' the Doctor said. 'All very secret, of course. You might not know about it . . .' He smiled. 'Yes. So we're from Head Office. I'm in charge of Health and Safety. Anyway, we're here to help.'

Amy looked confused. What was the Doctor talking about? She glanced at Rory, who shrugged.

The Doctor had taken out a small wallet and opened it to show the crew what was inside. It looked like blank paper behind a plastic covering, but Amy knew this was psychic paper – it showed people whatever the Doctor wanted them to see. If he had to pretend he had a ticket for travelling on a train or a bus, he could use the psychic paper. If he wanted to get into a top-secret army base, he could use the psychic paper. Like the sonic screwdriver, it was a very useful piece of kit.

'What are you a doctor of, exactly?' asked the captain.

'And who are you?' asked the Doctor, spinning round. He stared at the woman.

'I am Captain Jane Clancy.'

'Wonderful. Captain Jane! I like it.' The Doctor smiled. There was a small pause. 'Oh, I'm a doctor of almost everything. What's your mission here?'

'Don't you know?' asked Fleming.

'They didn't tell us about that,' said the Doctor. 'No time. They just sent us to keep an eye on things!'

'Really?' asked Fleming, looking a little nervous.

'We were just going to run through our last-minute checks for the drop,' Clancy replied.

'Drop?' asked Amy.

'The sub,' replied Fleming. 'You must know about that!'

'Of course we do,' the Doctor bluffed.

'Dropping a sub . . . submarine. Right?' asked Rory.

'That is what we do for a water planet like Hydron,' said Clancy.

'Thank you,' said the Doctor. He turned and pointed Amy and Rory to spare seats. They sat and listened as the captain told them about the mission.

'As you know, the planet Hydron is a world almost completely covered in water,' Captain Clancy explained. 'There are only a few rocky islands in the sea, and even those have freshwater lakes taking up most of the room on them. So, we can't build a normal base on the planet. Instead we have to use a submarine, which we've brought from Earth.'

'Ah! That's why the hold is so big!' the Doctor exclaimed.

'The submarine is an Under-sea Exploration Ship and its name is the *Ocean Explorer*,' said Clancy. 'The company has sent us to examine the freshwater lakes. According to my mission briefing, some interesting minerals have been detected there that we can use.'

'So you haven't been here before?' asked Amy.

'No,' Fleming said quickly.

'The company told me that the minerals were detected by a satellite.' Captain Clancy smiled. 'Anyway, the submarine will be dropped into the sea from space. The sub is protected against the heat of the planet's atmosphere. We will then use parachutes to slow us down before we hit the water. We don't expect there will be any difficulties.'

'Not before we get there,' muttered Fleming under his breath. The Doctor glanced at him but said nothing.

Clancy also looked at her security officer. Then she turned to Amy. 'Are you a marine expert?'

The Doctor jumped up again. 'She certainly is. With a name like Pond, she must know something about water.'

'It's not Pond,' said Rory. 'It's Williams.'

No one took any notice.

'I know quite a lot about the sea myself,' the Doctor said. 'Pescatons, Sea Devils, Skarasen, Myrka.' He lowered his voice. 'Even went to Atlantis once. Or was it twice? Anyway. Yes. You could say I'm an expert.'

'Good,' the captain said. 'We'll be leaving within the hour.'

The meeting came to an end. Captain Clancy stood up.

As her crew began to leave, another woman went up to Fleming. She wore white overalls and had her blonde hair pulled back into a bun. She whispered something to the head of security and then waved her arms about as if she was angry or perhaps scared.

'Don't worry, Doctor Morton,' Fleming said quietly but firmly. 'Nothing will go wrong.'

The Doctor watched the hushed conversation, then he followed Amy and Rory from the room. He caught up with his companions and together they followed the small team of people along a corridor to a lift. The lift took them down several decks until it opened on to the huge cargo hold.

Suspended from the ceiling and held by two giant metal clamps was the submarine. It was about the length of a football stadium and as tall as a house, with a tower that rose to a height of at least five metres above its hull. The tower had a thick metal door in its side that opened on to a ramp. A handful of crew members were carrying aboard the last few boxes of supplies for the mission. On top of the tower an engineer was adjusting the aerial that stood next to the periscope that was sticking out from the roof.

Although it looked like most submarines Amy had ever seen, the *Ocean Explorer* had large fins sticking out from either side at the back and front. More crew members dressed in blue stood on these fins or were suspended from scaffolding so they could carry out their last-minute checks.

'Wow,' said Amy.

'That's a big submarine,' added Rory.

'It is, isn't it?' the Doctor said with a smile. 'Let's get on board!'

An hour later, the Doctor, Amy and Rory were sitting in a large room at the front of the submarine. It was behind the sub's control room and Rory could see Captain Clancy and Fleming through the large hatchway that connected the two cabins. Like the others, Rory was strapped into one of the white leather chairs that lined the sides of the room.

He and Amy were wearing the yellow overalls they'd been given by the captain; the Doctor had also been given a pair, but had decided against donning them. Instead, he continued to wear his tweed jacket and bow tie. 'Bow ties,' he had explained to the captain, 'are cool.'

As he sat there, Rory counted the seats that lined the walls; there were forty. Apart from the people who had to be in the control room or the engine room, every other member of the *Ocean Explorer*'s crew was there. Most were wearing blue overalls, but there were quite a lot of people in black overalls, too; Rory wondered why a scientific mission needed so many security guards. He shrugged, then saw the woman who had been making a fuss earlier – Doctor Morton. She walked over to the chair next to Rory and sat down.

'Hello,' he said, looking sideways at the blonde.

She looked at him and smiled but said nothing.

'Right . . .' He smiled back. 'I'm Rory,' he continued. 'Are you a medical doctor?'

Finally she spoke. 'I am,' she said. 'Are you?'

'Oh. No. I'm a nurse. Well, I was,' he shrugged again. 'But then I've also been a Roman soldier and a security guard.'

'A Roman soldier?' she asked.

'It's a long story,' Rory said.

There was a pause.

'Well,' said Doctor Morton. 'If I need an assistant, I'll let you know.'

She turned and started speaking with the woman sitting on the other side of her.

'That went well,' Rory said quietly. He sighed. Before he could work out why Doctor Morton didn't seem to like him, an alarm began to sound. The crew all tensed.

'DOWN DROP IN TWO MINUTES,' said a computer voice.

Heavy thuds could be heard on the hull of the submarine as the giant claws moved it into position. Rory felt the spaceship bump a bit as it was jolted down. A low droning sound filled the room and he heard something like a rushing wind.

'They're opening the spaceship's outer doors,' the Doctor explained.

Rory nodded.

The alarm sounded again.

'DOWN DROP IN ONE MINUTE,' said the computer.

Amy looked at the Doctor and Rory. She had a big grin on her face. She blew out her cheeks then made an *eek* sound.

'It's not a fairground ride, Pond,' said the Doctor.

'Isn't it?' she asked cheekily.

'More like a parachute jump,' the Doctor said.

The alarm went off for a third time, and this time it didn't stop.

'DOWN DROP IN 30 SECONDS,' said the computer voice. 'RETRACTING FINS.'

There was a mechanical whine as the submarine's fins were pulled inside its main body. Everyone took this as a sign to grip the arms of their chairs in preparation for the drop. Rory gulped. He'd never done a parachute jump.

Then the computer started the final countdown, talking over the top of the noisy alarm: 'FIVE . . . FOUR . . . THREE . . . TWO . . . ONE . . . DOWN DROP!'

The Doctor grinned. 'Geronimo!'

# Chapter 2
# The Shoal

The claws released the submarine and it fell away from the *Cosmic Rover* like a brick dropped off a cliff. Rory's stomach lurched. He felt as if he was in the fastest lift ever built, descending from the top floor of the tallest skyscraper in the world to the basement.

The noise from outside was so loud Rory could hardly hear anything . . . except for Amy, that was. She was holding her arms up, shouting and smiling as if she was on a roller-coaster. The Doctor looked calm – almost a little bored. He'd obviously done this type of thing loads of times. Rory swallowed and closed his eyes tight shut.

Outside, the sub was starting to glow light orange as it fell. Then, as the sky around the ship turned from black to purple, the heat began to decrease. The submarine was travelling at well over a hundred miles per hour, zipping through the clouds of the planet Hydron.

Rory could feel the heat dying away now. He realised he had been holding his breath, and he slowly let the air out of his mouth. 'Phew!' he said and opened his eyes.

'PARACHUTES IN FIVE . . . FOUR . . . THREE . . .'

'Hold on!' the Doctor called over the noise of the wind.

'TWO . . . ONE!'

The submarine suddenly jerked; if it hadn't been for the seatbelts, Rory was sure he would have hit the ceiling of the room.

'DEPLOYING FINS,' the computer voice announced.

The Doctor smiled. 'It's okay, Rory. The fins will act like brakes. They'll slow us so we're ready for splash-down.' He gave Rory a thumbs-up.

In the calm waters of the purple sea far below, a creature rose to the surface. He looked like a strange sort of fish with flippers but he was larger than a man. His protruding eyes were enormous and his body was covered with brown and cream stripes. His name was

Makron and he was a member of the Shoal, the beings who lived on Hydron.

Makron turned his face to the sun and closed his eyes. The pattern of fins on his cheeks fluttered as they felt the sun's warmth. It was peaceful and relaxing. Then suddenly there was a whistling sound from above.

The Shoaly opened his eyes and saw a huge dark shape falling towards him. Above the shape were what looked like huge grey jellyfish – the submarine's parachutes. Makron's eyes widened in horror, and he dived back beneath the waves. He was terrified, and he had to tell his people about what he had seen.

Makron swam down through the purple water, passing many different creatures on his descent. Finally he reached the underwater kelp fields, which stretched away in every direction. Tall fronds of red and brown seaweed waved in the ocean currents. Makron could see several other Shoaly working in or travelling through the fields.

As soon as he had found the underwater road, he began to swim faster. The Shoal did not actually move along the seabed, so the roads on Hydron were simply a collection of coloured shells and stones on the ocean floor that acted as guides, leading the Shoal to different destinations. This road led to the Shoal's capital city, Reef.

Reef was a natural mountain of coral that had been carved and built upon by the Shoal. It was protected by a steep, hard rock face that was guarded day and night. Makron now approached the undersea cliff. The water had worn away at a crack in the stone to form a natural tunnel that served as the main entrance to Reef.

Two Shoaly were floating on either side of the tunnel entrance. These were the low swimmers – fish that had evolved deep in the oceans of Hydron – and they looked very different from Makron. These low swimmers were dark brown with grey stripes; they had huge mouths and strange golden eyes that looked like they were about to pop out of their heads.

The most unusual thing about them was their 'lure' – a small, glowing ball that hung from a piece of skin between their eyes. It could be used to hypnotise and, because its glow was caused by the low swimmers' natural electricity, it could also be used to stun or even kill other Shoaly.

Makron came to a stop and let the guards wave their lures over him, checking for anything odd or out of place. His cheeks pulsed an orange colour, telling the guards that he was in a hurry.

Like most Shoaly, the low swimmers did not wear many clothes, but they did have belts round their middles, from which hung two pieces of scanning equipment and a forked weapon. Since Makron was simply entering the city, there was no need for the guards to use the weapons or the scanners. A small flash of dull white on the nearest guard's face told Makron that he could pass.

Makron moved down the tunnel, overtaking other members of the Shoal: high swimmers like himself as well as medium swimmers, who were much more colourful. His father called them 'loud' and disapproved of them. Makron wasn't so sure about that, but it was his father he needed to see now.

The Shoal was looked after by the Assembly, which was made up of high swimmers, and Makron's father, Darkin, was a governor, one of the Shoaly in charge of a region. Makron had to tell his father what he had seen falling from the sky, and he knew exactly where his father would be.

The city of Reef was beautiful. It had no pollution and no square buildings. All of its structures were natural or had been built to look natural. The city was formed out of layers. The lower you went, the darker it became. That was where some of the low swimmers lived. Most of them lived outside Reef, deeper in the ocean in towns called Pools.

The highest point of Reef was a cone of bright orange coral decorated with different-coloured seaweeds, each representing one of the many regions of Hydron. This was where the regional governors gathered to talk about how to run the planet.

All the entrances to the Assembly building were guarded by dangerous-looking low swimmers. As Makron neared them, one flashed red at him – a warning. Then the low swimmer's face changed back to grey with a bit of yellow, telling anyone watching that this was a security check and that Makron should be careful. Makron slowed down and came to a stop in front of the low swimmers. Flashing a series of colours at the guards, Makron told them that he was in a hurry to see his father, who was a member of the Assembly.

One of the low swimmers took a scanner from his belt. It was triangular and shimmered like a butterfly's wing in all the colours of the rainbow. The guard scanned Makron with the device and it flashed white, confirming that his father did work there. The low swimmer nodded at Makron and the young Shoaly swam quickly past.

There were no doors in the Assembly building but most of the spaces between the arms of the coral had flat seaweed curtains so no one could see what was going on inside the rooms. Makron arrived at his father's office and burst through the curtain. His father was a large Shoaly with very clear stripes of light brown and dark cream.

*What are you doing?* his father asked, flashing red and black with anger.

Makron twinkled blue, green and pink. *I'm sorry, Dad.*

*Why have you rushed in here? What is so important?* Red, purple, black.

Makron paused. He wasn't sure his dad would believe him. He frowned. *They're back*, he said. Red: danger. Brown: return. Violet: alien!

The submarine hit the water and sank into the purple waves for a second before bobbing back up on to the surface and rocking slowly from side to side. The large grey parachutes that had slowed the submarine floated gently down. Two of them landed in the sea, while the third fell over the tower. It almost looked like the submarine had pulled a blanket over itself, ready for bed.

In the control room, Captain Clancy stared at the huge navigation screens and nodded. *Good.* They had made it. She turned to one of her crew and ordered him to bring the parachutes back in. He pressed a few buttons on his computer and the winch connected to the parachutes started to wind them in. As the parachutes were pulled back inside the sub, a special machine squeezed the water out of the material.

'Parachutes in,' said the sailor.

Captain Clancy nodded. 'Very good,' she said. 'Prepare to dive!' She turned round and found herself face-to-face with the Doctor.

'Are we in a hurry, Captain Jane?' he asked, looking at the navigation screens. 'I mean, there's a lovely purple sea out there. Couldn't we have a look at that first?'

'This isn't a tourist trip, Doctor,' she replied. 'We have a mission to complete. I need to get this submarine to one of the freshwater lakes as quickly as I can, and the report I was given before the mission said there were dangerous sea creatures here.'

'Did you say that the report was based on what a satellite found here?' the Doctor asked.

'That's right,' she said. 'It performed a scan of the planet and detected both useful mineral deposits and hostile life forms.'

'And the satellite was in space?' The Doctor came closer, peering at Captain Clancy.

She looked uncomfortable. 'Of course,' she said.

'So where is the satellite now?'

'I suppose the company must have collected it and taken it back to Earth.' Clancy smiled weakly. 'I'm just employed to do my job, Doctor, not to know all the ins and outs of how the company works.'

'Yes. I can see that,' the Doctor said. 'It's just interesting, isn't it?'

'What is?'

'That a machine in space can tell whether a creature under the sea is dangerous and hostile.'

Before Clancy could reply, a crew member interrupted her.

'All systems are ready, Captain,' the sailor said.

'Excuse me, Doctor,' Clancy said, and she walked away from him to talk to her crew. A man and a woman sat at the front of the control room, under the navigation screens – they were driving the submarine. Four others stood at the two side walls, pressing buttons to turn on the sub's engines.

'Not hanging around, then?' asked Amy. She walked up and stood beside the Doctor, and looked out at the strange sea.

'No,' the Doctor said. 'It looks like Captain Jane is in a hurry for some reason.'

'Ahead one third!' Clancy called. The crew members standing up started turning controls.

'Five degree down bubble!' called the captain.

'What on earth does that mean?' asked Rory.

Slowly, the floor of the *Ocean Explorer* began to tilt. Amy and Rory held on to each other so that they didn't fall over.

'It appears we're going underwater,' the Doctor said. He looked at Amy. 'I think we should investigate. There's something not right here. People are keeping secrets.'

The corridors in the submarine were painted white and had pipes running down them. They carried fresh water and air to all the cabins so that the crew could breathe, drink and wash. The Doctor walked alongside Rory and Amy, pointing to the different rooms they passed.

'At the front of the submarine is the control room,' he said. 'That sits over the sonar system.'

'Sonar is like underwater radar, right?' asked Rory.

'That's right,' replied the Doctor. 'They use it to see things like whales and other submarines and stuff.' The Doctor ducked under a particularly fat pipe. 'So, above the control room you have the sail – the tower that sticks up from the rest of the sub. That's where the periscope and radio antenna are. And where we are now is the mess,' he said as they walked into a large room filled with tables and chairs.

'Mess?' asked Amy. 'It looks tidy to me.'

'The mess is what the military or the navy call the kitchen and dining room.'

The Doctor sat down at one of the silver tables. Rory and Amy joined him.

'I don't know what's going on here,' whispered the Doctor. 'But I think we need to find out as much as we can from different people. I'll talk to Mr Fleming, the head of security, and I think you should stick with Captain Jane, Amy,' he said.

'What about me?' asked Rory, looking a little hurt.

'Don't worry. You are going to pay Doctor Morton a visit.'

'Oh,' said Rory, remembering that she didn't seem to like him. 'Great.'

# Chapter 3

# The Unexpected Visitor

The security centre was towards the back of the submarine. It was a large room containing numerous screens showing the feeds of cameras in different parts of the *Ocean Explorer.* There was a desk with computer controls, and a locked storage cupboard of weapons. In one of the side walls a doorway led to a group of four small cells. This was known as the 'brig'.

The Doctor entered the room and smiled at Fleming, who was sitting at the desk. The thin man looked up and frowned.

'Can I help you, Doctor?' he asked. It didn't sound like he meant it.

'I think you can!' The Doctor grinned. 'You see, I heard what you said to Doctor Morton during the meeting earlier.'

The Doctor walked round the desk and looked at the screens.

Fleming stood up. 'What do you mean?'

'Are you expecting trouble, Mr Fleming?' asked the Doctor. He didn't look at Fleming; instead he stared at a screen that showed Rory walking down a corridor.

'I am Head of Security,' said Fleming. 'It's my job to look for trouble.'

'Ah, yes. Well, I can understand that.' The Doctor turned to look at him now. He narrowed his eyes. 'But you're not looking for it. You know it's going to happen, don't you?'

Fleming opened his mouth to speak, but before he could say a word a warning sounded.

*Bleep! Bleep! Bleep!*

'See?' said the Doctor.

'It's the rear hatch!' Fleming snatched his gun from the desk and ran from the room. He shouted into a radio as he ran, 'Jason! Nick! Get to the rear hatch! Something's opening it!'

The Doctor nodded to himself, then he ran after Fleming.

Suddenly there was a loud *boom* from far away and the submarine lurched to one side. The Doctor was thrown against the wall, then fell to his knees. He looked up. 'Oh dear!' he said.

An alarm went off at high volume.

'HULL BREACH! HULL BREACH!' announced the computer voice.

The Doctor stood up and ran down the corridor towards the back of the submarine.

'This is the captain!' Clancy's voice came over the submarine's public-address system. 'Engineers, to the rear hatch. Crew, prepare to close the flood doors!'

The submarine lurched again, but this time the Doctor managed to stay on his feet. He jumped through a hatch and landed in water. It was about as deep as a paddling pool. Ahead of him, Fleming was talking to Rory outside the medical bay.

'What's happening?' called the Doctor.

'Doctor Morton has been attacked!' said Rory, pointing to a bunk in the medical bay where she was lying.

'Is she okay?' asked the Doctor.

Rory nodded. 'I scared off the thing that was attacking her.'

'You saw it?' The Doctor grabbed Rory by the shoulders. 'What did it look like?'

'He *says* he saw it,' said Fleming. 'We have only his word for that.'

'Are you suggesting that Rory attacked Doctor Morton?' asked the Doctor. 'Don't be ridiculous. This is my friend. He wouldn't lie.'

'Thank you,' said Rory.

'So, what did it look like?' the Doctor asked Rory, as he bent down and pulled the sonic screwdriver out from his jacket. It made a buzzing sound as he waved it over Doctor Morton's body. 'She'll live,' he said.

'It was big,' Rory said. 'Bigger than me. It looked sort of like a fish but it had great big bulging eyes. It was walking like a sea lion – on four things that looked like flippers, but the front ones had fingers.'

'Interesting,' the Doctor muttered. 'Come on!'

'Where are you going?' shouted Fleming.

The Doctor ran out of the door and sped up the corridor, splashing back through the water on the floor. 'It might still be on board!' he shouted back.

Rory and Fleming looked at one another. Rory shook his head. 'I'll stay here and look after the patient. You go!'

Fleming hesitated for a moment, then ran after the Doctor, catching him up just as he reached a closed door. A crew member stood beside it.

'When did you shut this?' demanded the Doctor.

'Just now,' replied the man, frowning.

'Well, open it again!'

'No!' Fleming looked at the Doctor. 'If we open that door, the submarine will be flooded. We'll sink.'

'We need to speak to that creature.' The Doctor looked at the man beside the door and then at Fleming. Neither of them moved.

'REAR HATCH SECURE. SUBMARINE SAFE,' the computer announced.

'Drain the seawater!' said Captain Clancy over the loudspeaker.

The Doctor shook his head and turned away from the door.

In the control room, Amy was watching the captain. She was impressed. Clancy had reacted well to the emergency. She had quickly given orders and made sure that the submarine was safe. Amy found that she liked the woman.

Then the Doctor marched in. His eyes flashed with anger. 'You know what is going on here and I demand to be told!' he said. 'Sea creatures do not open hatches and attack the crew for no reason.'

Captain Clancy looked at the Doctor as if he was mad. 'I don't know what you're talking about, Doctor,' she said. 'Really.'

'Captain, I think you and your entire crew are in danger and someone on board knows why.' The Doctor leaned forward and stared into her brown eyes. 'You can tell me,' he said gently.

Just then, Fleming entered the room. He looked first at the Doctor and then the captain. 'What's going on?' he demanded.

'That is exactly what I want to know, Mr Fleming,' the Doctor said. 'Why were we attacked just now?'

'Like the report says, this planet has hostile life forms,' Fleming said.

'Humans!' exclaimed the Doctor.

'I'm one, too,' Amy said, putting her hands on her hips. 'What have you done with my husband?'

'He's in the medical bay. He's looking after Doctor Morton. She was attacked by a fish creature.'

'Wow. Really?'

'Yes, really,' the Doctor said, looking over at Captain Clancy. His eyes narrowed and then he smiled. 'Captain Jane!'

She looked up at him.

'I want to have a look outside,' the Doctor said.

'What?' Amy and Clancy said together, then exchanged looks.

The Doctor explained that, because he was a very important person from Head Office, he could ask the captain of the *Ocean Explorer* to do whatever he wanted – as long as it didn't put the submarine in danger. 'I want to see what's out there,' he said. 'Or, rather, who's out there. If you've got fish creatures sneaking aboard, then I'd like to find out why.'

Fleming's eyes narrowed to slits, but he didn't say a word.

'Very well, Doctor,' Captain Clancy said. 'If you want to have a look outside, we can switch on the camera feeds and see from here.'

She moved over to a row of controls behind her chair.

'No,' said the Doctor. 'No, no, no. I don't want to watch TV. I'm more of a get-up-and-go sort of person than a sit-down-and-stop one. I want to get out there!' He pointed at the screen and the dark purple waters it showed.

'All right.' The captain sighed. 'Mr Fleming, show the Doctor to the *Verne*.'

The Doctor smiled. 'That's more like it!'

Amy rushed forward. 'I'm coming too.'

# Chapter 4
# Moon Pool

Fleming took the Doctor and Amy down a staircase in the corner of the control room. It was so steep, Amy thought, that it was more like a ladder than a flight of steps. They climbed down two decks and emerged into a large, brightly lit area.

There were cupboards and lockers against the walls. Amy could see orange diving suits hanging in the lockers along with bits of diving equipment. At the far end of the room, sitting on a platform, was a small yellow submersible that looked like it could fit about four people inside.

The most impressive part of the room, though, was what Fleming called the Moon Pool. It was a hole in the floor that opened straight on to the sea, so that part of the floor looked as though it was made of water.

The water didn't actually spill into the room, though; instead, its surface stayed level with the floor, just like that of a pool. Fleming explained that the air inside the submarine had to be kept at a certain pressure so as to stop the submarine from being crushed by the water around it; this meant that, so long as that pressure was maintained, the water could not get into the submarine through the pool.

Amy looked confused.

'Did you ever play with empty shampoo or bubble-bath bottles in the tub as a child?' asked the Doctor.

Amy nodded.

'You can hold a plastic bottle upside down in the bath with the cap off,' the Doctor explained. 'If you push the bottle down, the water doesn't get in. The air inside the bottle keeps it out.'

Amy looked at the Moon Pool. She found it hard to believe that the water didn't just rush inside and flood the submarine.

Fleming walked over to the yellow submersible, and the Doctor and Amy followed him. The small sub had a big round window at the front and several robotic arms on its sides. Amy thought it looked a little like a yellow crab. Then she noticed another sub behind it. She pointed this out to the Doctor.

'Yes, we have two submersibles,' explained Fleming. 'The bigger one is the *Verne* and the smaller one is the *Jules*.'

'One of my favourite writers,' the Doctor said, running a hand along the *Verne*'s smooth metal hull. 'He wrote *Twenty Thousand Leagues Under the Sea* – all about a submarine. Wonderful stuff. Very wild imagination. And that Nemo, eh? What a villain! Did you know that "Nemo" means "no one" in Latin?'

'Nemo?' asked Amy. 'Wasn't he a Disney character?'

'Not the clownfish!' the Doctor said. 'You can't have a clownfish in a submarine, sinking the world's sailing ships. That would be silly.'

'Obviously,' Amy said.

Fleming looked at them both oddly. 'You'll find diving suits over there,' he said. 'Change into them and then I can get you loaded into the *Verne*.'

Ten minutes later, the Doctor and Amy were dressed in orange diving suits and each carrying a helmet with a small light on the side. They climbed up the ladder on the side of the *Verne* and into the cockpit through a small airlock.

There wasn't much room inside the submersible. The Doctor and Amy took the two seats in front of the round windscreen. Behind them were two smaller seats but, since no one else was coming with them, Amy put her helmet there and the Doctor did the same. Then the Time Lord closed the hatch and screwed it tightly shut. There was a click as safety bolts locked the hatch.

'It's been a while since I drove one of these,' he said, wiggling his fingers.

Through the window, Amy watched as Fleming went to stand by a bank of controls. He pressed a button and spoke. 'Are you ready?' His voice came over the radio.

The Doctor pressed down his communication button. 'All set!' he said, grinning.

Fleming nodded and flicked some switches. There was a hiss as hydraulic arms pushed forward the platform on which the *Verne* was standing. Then, once the platform was completely over the Moon Pool, the hydraulic arms lowered the platform – and the sub – into the seawater.

Amy saw the water level rising. It reached the glass screen and then bubbled past until the sea closed over the sub.

'Okay,' said Fleming. 'You can keep in contact using the radio, but you're on your own now.'

'So we're looking for fish, then?' Amy asked the Doctor.

'Not fish, Amelia,' he replied, staring through the screen. 'That's like calling humans monkeys.'

'Okay, then. Fish people,' Amy said. 'Where do we find them?'

The Doctor looked at Amy and smiled. 'What is a fish's favourite party game?'

'What?' Amy frowned. 'Is this a joke?'

'Yes. What is a fish's favourite party game?'

'I don't know. Tell me.'

'Tide-and-seek!' The Doctor laughed and pushed the control stick down.

Amy shook her head. 'That is the worst joke I've ever heard,' she said, but she couldn't help smiling.

The Doctor's eyes twinkled. The *Verne* jerked away from the circle of the Moon Pool and dived down into the darker water below.

Rory was still in the submarine's medical bay. He was wearing a surgical mask and was looking at Doctor Morton as he held her wrist, taking her pulse. She was lying on a bunk, surrounded by a see-through plastic tent. Her breathing was fast, almost like that of a dog panting.

Rory bent down to look at Doctor Morton's face. She was sweating because of her high temperature. 'Can you hear me?' Rory said. 'I need to give you some medicine. Do you have anything for fever?'

Doctor Morton opened her eyes and licked her dry lips. 'Security pass,' she said and half lifted a hand in the direction of a desk and computer that sat on the other side of the room. Rory went over to it and found what looked like a credit card. It showed a picture of Doctor Morton with her name printed underneath – Rory saw that her first name was Angela.

'Is this it, Angela?' he asked.

She nodded her head once. 'Use it to open the cupboards,' she said.

Rory went over to the nearest medical locker. Below the handle there was a small panel. When Rory put the pass on the panel, the cupboard opened. Rory smiled. *Very useful*, he thought.

He quickly found the medicine cabinet containing the equipment he was looking for. He located a spray syringe and filled it with some medicine that he recognised, then made his way back to Doctor Morton and gently took her hand.

'I've found something to get your temperature down, Angela,' he said. 'It'll also help you to sleep.' He pressed the syringe against her arm. 'It will help your body to recover from the attack.'

Doctor Morton looked at him. 'Be careful,' she said.

Rory frowned. 'Don't worry,' he said. 'I'm a nurse, remember.'

She shook her head and whispered something. Rory thought it sounded like 'row'. Then she fell asleep.

Captain Clancy came into the medical bay.

'How is she?' the captain asked.

'I think she'll be okay,' Rory said. 'But I'm just a nurse.'

'Doctor Morton is the only medical officer on my crew,' Clancy told him. 'You are the best person to take care of her. Some of the crew know a bit of first aid, but you have proper medical training.'

Rory looked at her. There were plenty of crew aboard. There were main crew members and a lot of security guards. 'That's a bit mad, isn't it?' Rory asked. 'I mean, only one doctor? What would have happened if I wasn't here?'

'Well, there is a Robot Medic,' Captain Clancy said. She quickly explained that, if there was an emergency, every submarine had a robot that could be used. It wasn't programmed to do what a doctor could do, but it could help.

'Where is it, then?' asked Rory.

Ten minutes later, the robot was standing in the medical bay. Two engineers had brought it in and hurriedly assembled its three main parts.

The bottom bit looked like a tank; it was thick and heavy, because that was where the motor was, and it had a track on either side so it could move. The four small headlights at the front were switched off.

The robot's middle part was as wide as Rory's chest, and had lots of compartments where pills, medicines and tools were kept.

Above this were the robot's shoulders. It had two thin arms that each ended in three metal fingers. On its chest was a small computer screen, where medical information could be displayed. At the moment the screen was showing a green crescent moon that Rory guessed was the space equivalent of the Red Cross.

The machine's neck started at the height of Rory's waist. It was as thick as a lamp-post and jointed in several places. On top sat the Robot Medic's head; it had two large square lenses for eyes, and a small round speaker for a mouth.

'Greetings,' said the robot in a sing-song male voice. 'I am Medical Assistance Robot Vehicle for use in Emergencies. If it is easier, you can call me MARVE.'

The engineers left and Captain Clancy sat down at the small table. 'What exactly happened to Doctor Morton?' she asked.

'I'm not too sure, to be honest,' Rory said. 'But whatever attacked her left a nasty burn on her cheek.' He pointed to Doctor Morton's face, which was red from where something had hit her. 'By the looks of it, I think something gave her an electric shock.'

'What's the tent for?'

'That? Oh, well, it looks like the wound has an infection. I checked on the computer and it told me to put that up. It's called a Biological Hazard Tent.'

'Could it spread?' asked Clancy. She looked worried.

'I don't know,' said Rory. He was concerned, too. 'I'll be watching her very closely.'

'Thank you,' said the captain. 'I am sure you and MARVE here can keep things under control.'

She stood up and patted MARVE on the head, then left the medical bay. Rory looked at the robot. The robot looked at Rory.

'Are you just going to sit there?' asked the robot.

'What?' Rory stared at MARVE. 'Great! A robot with attitude. That's all I need.'

Several thousand metres away from where Rory was sitting, the *Verne* moved slowly through the dark purple depths of the sea. The Doctor was steering the submersible, peering through the window at the area of water ahead that was illuminated by the sub's headlights.

Amy was looking at a round sonar screen. On it, a yellow line swept round in a circle. Every time it found something larger than half a metre long or wide it made a loud pinging sound. The Doctor would then take the sub to have a look at whatever the machine had detected. So far they had found a rainbow-coloured jellyfish, a large crablike animal with ten legs, and a blob of floating water plants.

'Why was the sand wet?' he asked, still staring at the mass of kelp and other vegetation.

'Is this going to be another of your rubbish jokes?' Amy asked, folding her arms.

'Because the sea weed!' The Doctor looked sideways at her, a grin spreading across his face. Amy rolled her eyes, but smiled, too. She had to admit that one was quite funny.

Suddenly, without warning, the light in the *Verne* went off. All the power was gone. An orange emergency light came on and Amy grabbed the Doctor's arm.

'Steady, Pond,' he said. 'This might be just what we're looking for.'

Together they stared through the window, trying to see anything in the gloom of the waters outside.

There was a flash of bright red light a few metres away from the sub.

Amy jumped. 'What was that?' She sounded frightened.

Before the Doctor could answer, the first flash was joined by another, then another, and more until there was a whole army of pulsing red lights. In the glow they gave off, Amy could see that the lights belonged to a shoal of fish.

'They're making the lights flash with their skin,' Amy said quietly. 'How are they doing that?'

'Bioluminescence,' the Doctor replied. 'It's when an animal makes light by using the chemicals in its body. Like fireflies or glow-worms.'

'Or giant fish.'

'Deep-sea creatures on Earth can do it, too,' the Doctor said. He was staring at the light show like a toddler in a toy shop. 'It's beautiful.'

Then the fish charged.

Before the Doctor could answer, the first fish was joined by another, then another, and now suddenly there was a whole array of pulsing red lights. In the glow they gave off, Amy could see that the lights belonged to a shoal of fish.

'They're making the lights flash with their skin,' Amy said quickly. 'How are they doing that?'

'Bioluminescence,' the Doctor replied. 'It's when an animal makes light by using the chemicals in its body. Like fireflies or glow-worms.'

'Or these fish.'

'Deep-sea creatures on Earth can do it too,' the Doctor said. He was staring at the light show like a toddler in a toyshop. 'It's beautiful.'

Then the fish charged.

## Chapter 5

# The Cell in the Caves

In the medical bay, Angela Morton's condition was getting worse. The mark on the side of her face had turned from red to bright yellow. Worse, the infection had spread through her veins, covering her face in a pattern similar to a tree's root system.

Rory was now wearing a white biohazard suit with a hood, as well as a face mask, goggles, boots and gloves. Everything was sealed up so that he looked like he was wearing a spacesuit; this was so that the disease would not infect him too.

He climbed inside the plastic tent and stood beside the bed, looking with concern at Doctor Morton. Then he bent down and dabbed a small towel soaked in cold water on her face. Angela continued to murmur the word 'row' – or at least that's what it sounded like – in her sleep, but she did not wake up.

Rory wondered what she was talking about. Was she referring to a rowing boat? Did she want to row away from the submarine or something? He couldn't figure out what she meant, so he turned to speak with MARVE.

'It's an alien virus,' Rory said. 'Should we take a sample? Analyse it or something?'

'It would be a start,' MARVE replied.

'If I give it to you, can you look at it? Work out what it is and stuff?'

'Affirmative.'

Rory nodded. He removed a small plastic jar from his biohazard suit and unscrewed the top. Then he took a medical swab and wiped the material gently over Angela's face. He popped the swab back into the jar and screwed the top on again.

As he left the tent, he took off his hood with a sigh of relief, and passed the virus sample to MARVE. The Robot Medic took the jar with one of its thin metal hands, then moved over to the bench where various pieces of medical equipment sat. The robot put the virus sample into a machine that looked like a microwave and closed the door.

Just then, the hatch flew open and two crew members entered, carrying another man between them. They put the man on a bunk, and explained to Rory that he had collapsed in the engine room. Rory looked at the man's name tag: Luke Garlick. The man was trying to talk, but Rory calmed him down and rolled up his sleeve. Several yellow streaks ran up his arm from the wrist to the elbow.

Rory turned to the two men who had carried their friend in. 'It's spreading,' he said.

Quickly he contacted the captain on the radio and told her what was happening.

'You're the chief medical officer,' Clancy told Rory. 'What do we do?'

Rory thought for a second. He didn't know yet how the virus was spreading. Sometimes viruses spread by people touching surfaces or each other; the worst viruses were passed from person to person in the air – by people coughing and sneezing.

'Have any of the crew reported that they have colds?' asked Rory.

There was a silence on the radio while Captain Clancy thought about this. 'No. I don't think so.'

'Good.' Rory sighed. 'Then we can assume that the virus is spread through touch. We need to collect everyone who has touched Doctor Morton since the attack – including this man here,' he explained. 'Then we need to scrub this sub until it shines with anti-viral cleaner. Once we've done that we should be safe.'

'Should be?'

'Well, you see, Luke here might have touched walls or doors or bits of engine that other people have now touched too . . .'

'Are you saying that we don't have this under control?'

'Yes. That is exactly what I'm saying,' said Rory.

'Great,' said the captain.

'And there's one more thing,' Rory added.

'What's that?'

'I touched Doctor Morton when I carried her in here and put her on the bunk.'

'So you're infected?' Clancy gasped.

'I might be,' said Rory. 'I'll have to get MARVE to test me to see if I have got the virus.'

Rory switched off the radio and looked at the robot. 'If I get ill, are you ready to take over, MARVE?'

The robot's head bobbed up and down. 'Affirmative,' it said. Rory thought it looked as if MARVE was smiling.

Amy slowly opened her eyes. Her head hurt. A lot. It felt like someone had been playing the drums in her brain. She put a hand to her forehead and moaned as she sat up. She was no longer wearing the diving suit but was glad she still had yellow overalls on.

'Doctor?' She looked around her, and was startled to realise that she wasn't in the *Verne* any longer. Instead she was lying on the damp stone floor of a small cave that was lit with some form of glowing seaweed. Amy remembered the Doctor's silly joke and she gave a small smile.

Then she noticed an oval window and the smile slipped off her face. Beyond the glass was a really ugly creature. It had a wide mouth full of very pointy, very sharp teeth, and two huge golden eyes the size of footballs. The creature appeared to be holding a giant fork – whatever it was, it looked pointy, and Amy didn't want to find out if it felt as sharp as it looked.

She realised the cave must be some sort of cell and that the creature behind the glass was a guard.

'Doctor!' she called, louder this time.

A groaning noise came from behind her. Amy turned to see what was there, and was very relieved to see a body lying there wearing a tweed jacket. Unless the fish creatures had taken to wearing woollen clothes, she was pretty sure it was the Doctor.

'Ooh,' the Doctor said. 'Electrical overload. Causes the body and brain to shut down.'

'They knocked us out, you mean,' Amy said, and pulled the Doctor to his feet.

'Thank you. Yes. That is exactly what I mean. They knocked us out. So they don't want to kill us. At least, not yet.'

'Good,' Amy said. She was becoming impatient and wanted to go. 'Can we sonic the door, find the sub and get out of here?'

'Patience, Pond. We came here to speak with these creatures. They must be intelligent – they've built a cell especially for us. And that fish-guard-monster thing has a weapon, so they have technology.' He pointed to a basin beside the door with about ten large shells hanging beside it. 'They've even managed to get some fresh water for us, and they've provided something for us to drink from. Plus, they didn't kill us.'

'Yet,' said Amy.

The Doctor ignored his companion and walked past her to speak to the guard.

'Hello!' he said, wearing his best smile. 'Are you in charge here? Can we speak to you? There seems to have been a terrible mix-up.'

The fish creature seemed to frown at them.

'I don't think he likes us,' said Amy.

'No,' said the Doctor. 'It's not that.' He stared at the guard for a few seconds, then he hit his forehead with his palm. 'Of course! Fish! Remember the Hath, Amy? Oh no, that wasn't you . . .'

'The Hath?'

'Doesn't matter. The point is they're fish.'

'Well spotted,' said Amy.

'Fish don't talk.'

'Duh,' said Amy. 'Of course fish don't talk!'

'Well, actually, they do, just not like you and I. The Hath had bubbles – most fish don't make any sound, but they do communicate,' the Doctor said. 'Look at this chap. Look closely at his face, Amy.'

Amy did as she was told. The creature was not pretty to look at, but she stared really hard at its face. As she did so, she leaned nearer and nearer to the window. Suddenly the fish's face lit up with a flash of red.

Amy jumped back. 'It's the same type of fish thing that attacked the submersible earlier,' she said.

'And?'

Amy looked blank for a few seconds, then she realised. 'It can change the colour of its skin!'

'Exactly!' The Doctor beamed. 'Now, normally the TARDIS can translate any language, but this is a little on the odd side. The TARDIS can't help us with this. No. We need to find a way to say hello to Mr Anglerfish here.'

He spun round on the spot and walked a few paces to the back corner of the cell. His hands were clasped together with both index fingers sticking out and touching. Amy knew that he was deep in thought. Then his fingers began to wiggle. Amy knew this meant he had come up with a plan – or was about to.

'Creating colour from nothing. I mean, it's not easy, is it?' the Doctor said. 'We have your clothes. My clothes.'

'I am *not* taking my clothes off!' said Amy indignantly.

The Doctor shook his head. 'No, no, no. I just need a piece of them. A bit of your yellow overalls.'

'A bit? You mean you're going to cut up my overalls?' Amy looked defiantly at the Doctor. 'No way!'

'Oh, stop moaning,' the Doctor said, taking the sonic screwdriver from his pocket. 'I'll get you some new ones.'

The sonic screwdriver buzzed and the Doctor quickly cut a square the size of a potato crisp from the side of Amy's overalls.

'There!' he said.

Then he cut a piece the same size from the red top Amy was wearing beneath her overalls, before moving on to his own clothing. The sonic quickly cut a square out of his greeny-brown jacket and another from his black trousers at the ankle.

'Now we just need some way of mixing them,' he said.

'And we don't know what the colours mean,' Amy reminded him.

'Ah,' the Doctor said and stared at the little pieces of material in his hand, as if the pieces themselves were about to tell him what they meant.

Just then, the cell door opened and two fish guards entered. They walked on their back two fins as if they were feet. One of the guards held his three-pronged weapon out before him to keep the Doctor and Amy at bay. Behind them was a different fish person. He was much lighter in colour and had smaller eyes with humanlike black pupils.

'I think you'd better work it out fast!' Amy squealed.

# Chapter 6
# The Locked Door

Rory looked up from the patient he was tending to and saw MARVE pushing a floating stretcher with a man on it into the medical bay. This new patient was moaning and the telltale signs of the yellow virus showed on his skin. There were only six beds in the room, and five were already occupied; with the new arrival, the medical bay was now full.

Rory didn't know what he would do if anyone else got sick. He would have to see what extra space there was nearby. He didn't really want to talk to the captain about it, as their last conversation had not ended well . . .

MARVE had tested him for the virus, and he had been pleased to learn he wasn't infected. So he had gone to the control room to report on the virus and what he was doing to cure the crew. There with the captain were Mr Fleming and two security guards – again, Rory was surprised at how many guards there were. He wasn't sure he trusted anyone on board the sub, and what Captain Clancy said next didn't do anything to change his mind.

'I'm afraid we've lost contact with your friends.'

Rory was concerned but not surprised. 'When?' he asked.

Fleming replied, 'When we send out a submersible, we always keep an eye on it.' He pointed to a screen on one of the *Ocean Explorer*'s control panels. 'Each submersible sends out a signal so that we can always find it. The *Verne*'s signal stopped broadcasting forty-five minutes ago.'

'What does that mean?' Rory frowned. He didn't like the sound of that.

Clancy and Fleming looked at each other.

'Well,' said Clancy. 'The best we can hope for is that there is some natural reason why we can't pick up the signal, such as some kind of chemical or tidal disturbance in the water. It's rare, but it does happen.'

'Or they might have taken the sub into a cave of some sort,' Fleming said. 'If it was under the seabed, we wouldn't be able to pick up the signal. Or if they were out of range, but that's not likely.'

'And what if they aren't in an underwater cave or in a chemical cloud or whatever?' asked Rory. 'Does that mean . . . ?' He didn't want to finish the question.

Clancy came forward and put a hand on his shoulder. 'It could mean that the sub has suffered a power failure or that it has sunk or . . .' She hesitated. 'Or it may mean the *Verne* has been destroyed.'

Rory shook his head. 'No,' he said. 'No. I don't believe that. The Doctor wouldn't let that happen.'

'I'm sorry,' said Fleming.

'So what do we do about it?' asked Rory. 'They might need help!'

'I'm sorry, Rory,' Captain Clancy said. 'But we don't have time –'

'Don't have time? Are you kidding?' Rory shouted. 'That's my wife and my friend you're talking about.'

'We have a mission to complete,' Fleming said. 'It's very important and we can't hang around.'

'My wife's life is very important,' Rory hissed. 'The Doctor's life is very important. Any life is.' He faced the captain. 'If you want my help with this virus, you'd better find a way to "hang around" and look for them.'

Clancy had held up her hands. 'Okay, look. We'll launch a rescue buoy.'

'What good will that do?' asked Rory.

'A rescue buoy is a floating pod that has emergency food and water supplies,' Fleming explained. 'It also has a radio, so the Doctor and Amy can contact us if their own radio is damaged. The pod can also be sealed off from the sea so that it is warm and dry if they need to stay there for a while.'

'The rescue buoy will send out a signal to the *Verne*,' Clancy added. 'If the sub is damaged and has any power left, the pod will bring it to the surface using autopilot.'

Rory nodded. He didn't believe for one second that the Doctor and Amy were dead, but if they were in trouble he wanted to be sure that he had done everything he could for them. 'Okay,' he said. 'You'll do that now?'

'Right away,' Clancy said. 'Mr Fleming, will you make sure the buoy is launched from the Moon Pool immediately?'

'Yes, ma'am.' Fleming saluted and left the control room.

'Can I still depend on your support in the medical bay?' asked Clancy.

'Yes,' Rory said, then added, 'And I think I'd better get back there.' He had hurried out of the control room and back to the medical bay.

That had been half an hour ago.

Now, Rory was rushing around giving medicine to six crew members and hoping that it would work. It was difficult, because he had run out of plastic tents so he had to wear his biohazard suit all the time. No one else was allowed in the medical bay, and only MARVE was permitted to pick up crew members who developed the virus.

Everyone else on board was wearing gloves and surgical masks that made them look like doctors in an operating theatre. Rory knew they were all afraid; no one wanted to catch the virus.

Rory sighed. No matter what was going on elsewhere on the submarine, he had a job to do. Right now, that was looking for more room in case anyone else got sick. Rory had a nasty feeling that was definitely going to happen.

There was an uncomfortable silence in the cell. The new arrival – a far more attractive-looking fish than the two guards – stared at the Doctor. The Doctor was busy miming, trying to say hello, and introduce himself and his companion. He even tried to wave the coloured squares that he had cut from his and Amy's clothing.

'I don't think that's working,' said Amy.

'Shhh.' The Doctor held a finger to his lips. 'If they don't use sound to communicate, they might find it strange or impolite if we do.'

'Tough,' said Amy.

The Doctor looked at her. 'Please, Amelia.'

'All right,' she whispered, and she stood back to allow the Doctor to continue his efforts.

'I think I'm starting to understand some of what they're saying when they flash different colours,' the Doctor explained in a whisper. 'But I think we've got a long way to go yet.'

Makron watched the strange creatures through the cell window. He found them a bit frightening but funny at the same time. Makron had decided that the pink creature with the brown hair on its head was in charge, and the one with the long orange hair was its friend or helper. He also assumed that the one with brown hair, because of its bone structure and size, was male.

When they started making noises at each other, Makron almost laughed. He could see his father's face, and it was clear that his father did not think it was funny at all. Then the one with the brown hair started using his coloured squares again.

He held up the green one first and then pointed at different things in the cell: the basin, the one with the orange hair, the guard. Then he made a movement with his shoulders that made his neck look shorter. Makron had no idea what he was doing.

His father moved forward, changing the colour of his skin to ask the question, *What are you doing here?*

The male creature was staring at Darkin. Then he smiled and lifted a hand to wave his fingers around by Darkin's face. Makron could see this didn't please his father, but he stayed still. Then the male pointed to his own face and shook his head. He held up a piece of red material.

Was he saying that his face hurt? Then Makron realised something: the creature was trying to talk. He bashed the long fins of his hand on the window. His father and the two low swimmers turned round to look at him.

*They're trying to talk to you!* Makron said.

*What do you mean?* asked Darkin. *Why don't they talk normally?*

*They can't*, Makron said. *They can't change their skin colour. The male is trying to use the cloth.*

Darkin ordered the guards to let his son in, then he turned back to the prisoners. He pointed at them and flashed violet. *You're aliens*, he said.

The male prisoner nodded and held up the black square of material.

*He's asking if you're in charge, I think*, Makron pulsed.

Darkin flashed his cheeks white for a second and bobbed his head. *Yes.*

The male clapped his hands together and started making noises to the female. Darkin's face went a little red with annoyance. The Shoal did not make sounds, so they did not think it was polite for others to do so.

Makron sighed. His father didn't understand. These were aliens. Everything they did would seem odd to the Shoal. It must be the same for them.

The Doctor was smiling, his eyes narrowed with happiness.

'Okay, clever clogs,' Amy said. 'You managed to say hello to the fish people! Now what?'

'Now we can explain that we're friendly and they can let us go,' the Doctor said.

'I've heard that before,' Amy replied.

'Well, this time it will work,' the Doctor said a little sadly. 'I'm sure it will.'

'Go on then,' Amy said, and waved him back to his conversation with the fish creatures.

Aboard the *Ocean Explorer*, Rory had found a short side corridor just along the main passage from the medical bay. It was narrow and not very well lit. He hesitated, looking down the corridor, then tentatively took a step forward as if the floor was alarmed and if he trod too hard, sirens would go off all over the submarine.

Nothing happened. He sighed with relief and nodded his head. *Yeah, this will be all right.* He took another step, then stopped. There was a door in the wall to his right. It had a small round window in it, but there appeared to be a shutter on the inside covering the window.

As far as Rory could tell, this corridor was next to the medical bay, but the medical bay only had one door into it. So where did this door go?

Rory returned to where the side corridor joined the main passageway. He walked steadily back to the medical-bay door, counting his paces. It took him twelve strides. Then he entered the medical bay and counted his steps from the door to the far wall. It was only eight.

That couldn't be right. Unless there was another room there.

Rory quickly returned to the T-junction in the corridor and looked about to ensure he hadn't made a mistake. No. He had come out of the medical bay, turned right, walked down the passage and found this little corridor, also on the right. He frowned. *I suppose*

*I'd better check out what's behind the door,* he thought. If it was another room, it would be the best place to put any extra crew members who got sick.

Dipping his hand into his pocket, Rory brought out Doctor Morton's security pass. He slowly reached forward to put the pass on the panel beneath the door handle.

'Can I help you?'

Rory jumped and dropped the card. It was Fleming. He was standing in the main corridor looking down the side passage. He had one hand on the holster where he kept his gun.

'Sorry,' Rory said. Why did he say that? He shook his head. 'I was, um, looking for some more space. You know, for the patients. Not space like outer space. Space like room. For extra beds.'

'Well, you won't find it down there.'

'Really?' Rory asked. 'I thought this door might lead to another room. I mean, it's a bit strange but . . .'

Mr Fleming walked towards him. 'It's just a cupboard,' he said.

'Of course,' Rory said. 'Just a cupboard.' He held out his hand and grasped the door handle. Mr Fleming moved forward suddenly, as if to stop Rory, but the door was locked.

'Locked,' said Fleming. 'As it should be.' He lifted Rory's hand off the door handle. 'It's a security cupboard,' he explained, dropping Rory's hand.

'Right.' Rory looked down. 'Nothing special.'

'That's right,' Fleming said with a smile. He seemed relieved that Rory understood. Then the smile faded as he saw something on the floor. The security officer bent down and picked up Doctor Morton's security pass.

'What are you doing with this?'

'I needed it to unlock the lockers in the medical bay,' Rory explained.

'Did you now?' Fleming looked at Rory as if he was suddenly a threat. 'Are they still unlocked?'

'Yes.'

'Then you don't need this any more, do you?'

'I suppose not,' Rory said. He was still standing by the door. Fleming beckoned him back to the main corridor.

Rory hesitated. Should he say something? Oh well . . . 'Why would you put a window in a cupboard door? And then why would you put a shutter over the window on the inside?'

Mr Fleming stepped up to Rory so that they were face-to-face. Rory managed not to move even though he felt scared of the other man.

'It's a security matter,' said Fleming. 'Forget about it.'

Rory nodded. 'Sure,' he said.

'Now return to the medical bay,' the security officer hissed. 'And stay there. I will see if we can find you another room for the patients. Got it?'

Rory bobbed his head again. 'I understand,' he said and walked back to the medical bay.

The Doctor was right. There was something strange going on, and it had something to do with that cupboard.

Mr Fleming might have taken Doctor Morton's pass but Rory had a plan to find out what was in there.

## Chapter 7

# Colourful Language!

When the Doctor was excited he looked a bit like a meerkat or a squirrel – darting about the place with bright eyes. Amy thought that if he had a tail, it would definitely be bushy and twitching.

The Doctor had realised that he needed many more colours to be able to talk to the fish creatures. He seemed to be happiest when he had to think quickly and make stuff up on the spot.

While the Doctor busied himself waving bits of clothing at the fish people, Amy checked out the cave they were in. The rock of the back wall was quite uneven, with different types of seaweed growing in small clumps here and there – Amy realised that the cave must be underwater usually, or the seaweed couldn't survive in it. The fish creatures must have drained the water from it so that she and the Doctor could breathe. She hoped that whatever the Doctor was doing would work, because she didn't want to be in the cave cell if the fish people changed their minds and let the water back in.

She stood with her arms folded and watched the Doctor run to the basin and grab the shells that they were supposed to use for drinking. He filled five of them with water and left the others empty. Then he put all of them on the floor of the cave, in between him and the four fish people, and took out the sonic screwdriver.

Immediately the guards moved forward with their weapons, but the fish creature in charge ordered them back. They stood by the door, holding their weapons at the ready.

The Doctor didn't seem to notice. He started waving the sonic screwdriver over all of the different types of seaweed growing on the wall. Suddenly he bent down, put the sonic in his mouth and plucked at one of the plants, grabbing as much of it as he could. Then he dashed back to the row of shells and dropped an equal amount of the plant into the middle three.

'What on earth are you doing?' Amy asked.

'Hydron, Amy. We're on Hydron. Not Earth,' the Doctor mumbled. He still had the sonic screwdriver clenched lengthways between his teeth.

'Yup,' said Amy. 'I know where we are. Why are you running about picking seaweed?'

The Doctor looked up at her and smiled. 'It's a pH indicator,' he said.

'A what?'

'It tells you how much acid something has in it,' he explained. 'Didn't you ever do this at home?'

'Nope.' Amy wasn't impressed.

'Well, on Earth you'd use red cabbage, probably. Fortunately there's some form of sea kale here that contains the same ingredient as red cabbage – it's called flavin. Anyway, if you boil it up in water, it will change colour when you add stuff to it.'

Amy smiled. He was the maddest, most brilliant person she had ever met. 'So how do you boil the water –'

Before she could finish what she was saying, the Doctor had pointed the sonic screwdriver at the first shell and switched it on. As the sonic buzzed away at a high pitch, the water started to bubble, then boil. Thin clouds of steam floated up towards the ceiling. The Doctor's smile got wider.

The fish creatures were also watching the Doctor. They seemed just as amazed and fascinated by the Doctor as Amy was. He had this effect on most people.

Soon the Doctor had a row of shells with boiling water and seaweed in them. As Amy watched, the plants started to turn the water a dark pink colour. Then he put the sonic away and started patting his pockets and pulling all manner of things from them. He had a small ball of string, a tangerine, a stick of chalk, a handful of paper clips and a tiny sachet of tomato ketchup.

The fish creatures looked at one another.

Ignoring the funny looks he was getting, the Doctor quickly peeled the tangerine. He squeezed the juice from it into the farthest shell. Then he tore open the tomato ketchup and added it quickly to the nearest seashell. Finally he took the piece of chalk, broke it into pieces and added it to the middle shell. Then he whipped out the sonic screwdriver again and dipped it into the water cups one at a time.

'Usually you'd have to wait a little bit for this to work, but we need to speak with these people quickly!'

Amy saw that the contents of the three shells were changing colour. The one with the ketchup in it became yellow, while the one with tangerine juice had gone a brilliant red. The shell with the piece of chalk in it was turning a dark blue.

'So now we have three colours,' Amy said. She was still confused. 'Didn't we have three colours of material anyway?'

'Watch, Pond!' The Doctor picked up the yellow and the blue. 'These three are primary colours, which means we can do this!' He poured a little of each into one of the empty shells and stood back. One shell now had green water in it. He quickly mixed purple, orange and brown. He left one shell with clear water in it.

'And the material is still useful!' The Doctor held up the square of black he had cut from his trousers, then placed it in the last shell that had water in it. He applied the sonic screwdriver, which boiled the water with a buzz. In the steaming water, the black colour ran from the cloth, turning the water black, too.

'There!' the Doctor said. He stood back and admired his handiwork. He had a full rainbow of colours as well as black and transparent. 'Now we can have a proper conversation!'

Back on the *Ocean Explorer*, Rory was feeling very pleased with himself. Mr Fleming might have taken Doctor Morton's security pass, but Rory knew exactly where to get another one; a patient who had been brought into the medical bay earlier was a security guard. Not only was Rory pleased with himself for realising that the security guard would have a pass, but he was also happy because he had worked out that a security guard could go anywhere.

While MARVE was looking after one of the other sick crew members, Rory moved over to where the security guard was sleeping. He checked to make sure that the robot wasn't watching, then he searched the man's pockets for the pass. Sure enough, he found it in the left-hand jacket pocket. Rory quickly slipped the pass into his own pocket, then told the robot he was going to the bathroom.

He headed out into the corridor and made for the side passage. He quickly walked up to the door with the round window in it, pressing the security pass against the panel under the handle and pulling the door open.

Beyond the door the room was dark, but Rory could see it was bigger than a cupboard. The room had two rows of large glass tubes that looked a little like the one on top of the TARDIS's control console. The tubes were about the width of a dustbin and were full of water. A strange blue light lit these tubes from underneath, and inside each Rory could see a dark circle the size of a football.

Rory stepped into the room and moved to look at the nearest tube. Small bubbles were coming from the bottom of the cylinder as if the water inside was being kept full of air – like a pump does in a fish tank. He stared at the dark footballs and wondered what they could be. Then he caught sight of a shape against the light. There was something inside the football.

He moved back to the door and hunted about for a light switch, but as he was doing so he spotted a workbench against the far wall. On the bench, lit by a single spotlight, was a large plastic container. Rory frowned. Why was it under a spotlight?

*It must be important*, he thought, so he went over to take a closer look.

As he neared the container, he thought he could smell something; when he took the lid off the plastic box he could see why. The stink of fish was overpowering. He had to put a hand over his nose and mouth to stop himself from being sick.

Slowly, he looked into the box. At first he thought it was seaweed. Whatever it was, it appeared to be rotting. Yuck! Rory looked away again. Then he told himself it was okay and plucked up the courage to take another look.

It was just a lump of stuff, like a flap of skin – in fact, it looked just like a deflated black football, only slimier. That was when he realised what the things in the tubes were: baby fish. Rory turned round and looked at the glowing glass containers. The dark shapes hanging in each one were not balls – they were fish eggs!

Rory knew there was a special word for fish eggs. He scratched his chin as he thought. *Fish roe!* That was it! Then his hand fell away from his face. *Roe.* That was what Doctor Morton had been saying, not 'row'. The two words sounded the same, but she must have been talking about the fish eggs. What's more, the room was right next to the medical bay.

So Doctor Morton had been trying to warn Rory about the fish eggs. But why? And the thing in the box wasn't really a whole egg; it was just the outer covering. Not a shell, because fish eggs don't have shells. It was more like a case or a seedpod.

Rory wondered what the eggs were doing there. The submarine had only just arrived on the planet, and no one had been outside of it except for Amy and the Doctor. Why had Mr Fleming been so keen to hide the eggs from Rory? Were they going to let the eggs out into the sea on Hydron? Was it like returning captive animals to the wild or something?

There was only one way to find out. Rory would have to ask the captain.

He marched away from the workbench and back out into the passage. He had just pulled the door shut behind him when all the lights on the submarine went out.

The power was down.

Then Rory noticed that not only was there no light, but the air pumps had stopped working too. They'd suffocate! The darkened sub lurched suddenly and Rory realised he was wrong. They wouldn't suffocate. They'd never get the chance, because without power the submarine was sinking. Fast.

# Chapter 8

# The Water Volcano

Rory stumbled out along the side corridor and into the main passage, hitting his head against the metal wall as he went. An alarm sounded and red emergency lights bathed the submarine in a strange crimson glow that made it look like a small area of hell. Rory checked his head, and it wasn't bleeding. He'd live.

The *Ocean Explorer* swayed violently to one side, sending Rory falling once again, this time against a bulkhead wall. In the same moment, a rushing noise like a leaf blower or a really big fan filled the ship. Rory was sitting down now so when the submarine tipped to one side at an angle it didn't affect him as much.

Rory had to find out what was going on.

He stood up carefully and stretched out his arms so that his hands were pressing against both sides of the corridor. Then he started to walk, using his arms to brace himself against any sudden movement. He reached the meeting area behind the control room and stepped through the hatch that led from the corridor. Then he noticed that the whole sub had angled upward. They weren't sinking any more; they were surfacing.

Captain Clancy was gripping the arms of the leather command chair very tightly. Everyone was watching the depth gauge, which seemed to be working despite the power failure. Rory could see it ticking quite quickly towards zero.

Rory reached the captain's chair. 'What happened?' he asked.

Clancy didn't look at him. 'I don't know,' she replied quietly. She was watching the depth gauge intently, as the numbers ticked down: 24 . . . 23 . . . 22 . . .

'We lost power across the ship. Our engines just stopped working. Luckily we've got a small back-up generator.' Finally she tore her eyes away from the gauge and looked at Rory. 'That gave us the power to blow the ballast tanks so that the sub could surface. I just hope we blew enough air into them to reach sea level.'

'Blow the tanks?' he asked. The depth gauge continued to count down: 14 . . . 13 . . . 12 . . .

'The *Ocean Explorer* is just a metal tube full of air, really,' Captain Clancy said. 'To go underwater, the submarine has to make itself heavier. So we have special tanks that are filled with water to make the sub go down, and then if we want to go up they're blown full of air, which pushes the water out of them.'

'Right,' Rory said. He looked back at the digital read-out: 5 . . . 4 . . . 3 . . . 2 . . . 1 . . .

The numbers on the gauge approached zero and, at the same time, the floor of the sub levelled out.

'Looks like we made it!' Clancy jumped out of her chair, took some binoculars from a junior crew member, and ran towards a hatch at the back of the control room.

'Where are you going?' asked Rory.

'Up top, for a look. You coming?'

'Sure!' Rory followed her to the hatch, then up a ladder to another level and another hatch, this time above their heads. Clancy started turning the small wheel on the hatch to open it, then she pushed up with a grunt of effort. The hatch door swung open, letting a shower of water in. Rory jumped back, but Clancy ignored it and climbed the last ladder out on to the top of the submarine's tower.

Rory emerged from the hatch after her on to a slippery metal deck about the size of a double bed. It was just wide enough for Clancy and him to stand side by side. She was leaning on the low metal wall that ran all the way round the top of the tower. At the back of the wall was a gap where a ladder descended from the top of the tower down to the main part of the sub's outside deck.

'There!' said the captain, pointing. Even without binoculars, Rory could see that there was an island ahead of them. He guessed it might be about fifteen kilometres away. He wasn't very good with distances.

'I thought there wasn't any land on this planet,' he said. 'You know, you said it was a water world . . .'

'There are islands,' she replied. 'But they're more like steep mountains sticking out of the ocean. You can't build anything on them. You'll see.'

'Will I?'

'Yes. We're going to that island. That's where the company wants us to go, so that's where we're going.'

'But what's there?' Rory asked.

'My report says there is a mineral in the lake that we can use for power.'

'But we don't have any power right now,' Rory observed.

'We've got enough to get us there.'

'And then what?'

'Then, we'll see, won't we?'

***

In the cave cell, the Doctor seemed to be making progress. He was slowly learning what the colours that he had in each shell could mean. He had taken off his jacket and was sitting on the floor with his legs crossed.

'These fish people have a very complicated way of talking,' Amy said. 'Won't it take forever just to say one sentence?'

The Doctor shook his head. 'They're not fish people, Amy,' he said and smiled at the group in front of him. 'As far as I can understand, they are called the Shoal.'

'The Shoal?'

'Yes. It means a group of fish – like a herd of cows or a flock of birds.' The Doctor paused for effect. 'A shoal of fish.'

He pointed to his most recent addition to the shells. It had diluted black water in it. 'That's grey, by the way. Grey means *together* or *group*, as well as *strength*. I think. Anyway I am guessing they call themselves the Shoal and that an individual is a Shoaly or a Shoalite. Shoaly, I think.'

Amy frowned. 'It doesn't sound very clear to me,' she said.

'It's not.' The Doctor grinned. 'Like you say, it's very complex. When they use colour they sometimes move their cheek fins at the same time.' His grin faded. 'I can't do that.'

'Aww, poor Doctor,' Amy joked. 'Can't move his cheek fins!' She laughed.

The Shoaly stared at Amy. The Doctor shushed her.

'Don't make silly noises, Amy,' the Doctor hissed. 'Remember? They think it's rude.'

Amy pouted her lips. 'So does your colourful water display mean you can tell them we aren't baddies and that they can let us go?' she whispered.

'I'm working on it,' the Doctor said in a low voice and returned his attention to the Shoaly.

He pointed at the blue and then the yellow.

'Are you trying to tell them how to make green?' Amy asked with an eyebrow raised.

'Amelia!' The Doctor sighed quietly. 'Very well. I will explain it to you. I am saying *peaceful* and then *friend*. I hope.'

The larger of the two Shoaly that looked like lion fish turned his cheek blue and then yellow in reply.

'There! You see?' The Doctor smiled again.

'Oh yeah!' Amy was impressed. 'Can you ask them for a cup of tea?'

'One step at a time,' the Doctor whispered. 'We have to take care. If I point at the wrong colour, I might offend them.'

'You mean, you might say naughty words in fish language?' Amy giggled softly.

The Doctor ignored this and started pointing at the shells again, explaining as he did so what he hoped he was saying to the Shoal.

The wind ruffled Rory's hair as he leaned on the tower's handrail. The *Ocean Explorer* had taken about an hour to cover the fifteen kilometres to the island. In the meantime, Rory had gone back down into the sub and met with Mr Fleming. The security officer had shown him a spare bunk room to use for any extra patients. This was lucky, because two more crew members had come in with signs of the yellow virus.

Rory had decided not to say anything about the strange fish roe he had found in the lab behind the medical bay. He thought that Fleming would probably lock him up – or worse – if he told anyone what he had seen. He knew that Fleming and Morton were in on it, and he wondered if Captain Clancy was too – but he would have to wait to find out.

Besides giving the new patients medicine to help them sleep, there wasn't much more Rory could do for them. He hoped that, by sleeping, the sick crew members would be able to fight off the virus. MARVE was now monitoring their vital signs to make sure their conditions didn't get any worse. So far none had, but they hadn't shown any signs of getting better either. Rory was a nurse. What he really needed was a doctor. Or better still, *the* Doctor!

From where he stood at the tower now, Rory could see up ahead the huge mountain of the island. It was massive. It reached into the purple clouds like a skyscraper, thousands of metres high. He couldn't see the top because it was hidden in the clouds. The sides of the mountain rose almost vertically from the ocean, like cliffs. Whatever that satellite report had said, it was right about one thing: there was no way of building anything on this island. There was no flat land at all.

'Having fun, Mr Williams?'

Rory looked round. It was Captain Clancy. He smiled. 'Tell me again. Why have we come here?' he asked.

The captain explained that before her team had come to Hydron she had read the report on the planet. She had learnt about the islands, and that – amazingly – there was a lake at the top of each mountain.

'A lake?'

'Yes. We think the islands may be water volcanoes,' Clancy said. 'On each island, the lake at the top is linked to the sea below by a network of underground tunnels. The water flows down from the lake through these tunnels.'

'So how does the water get up there in the first place?'

'In the same way water gets about on Earth – it rains.' Captain Clancy pointed up at the purple clouds.

'So the lake is freshwater?'

'Yes,' Clancy smiled. 'But that's not why we are here. The report says that we can use something in the lake as fuel for our engines.'

As she spoke, the submarine entered the shadow cast by the huge water volcano. Rory shivered because of the slight temperature drop.

'But how do we get up there?' he asked.

'We climb.'

## Chapter 9

# Admiral Icktheus

A short distance from the Assembly building in Reef was a darker, more forbidding one. It was carved from grey coral rather than the orange of the other structures. Bright red seaweed floated from its roofs and towers, telling every member of the Shoal that this was the base of the low swimmers.

The low swimmers had always been the guardians of the Shoal. No other swimmer was allowed to join their ranks. Only the low swimmers, with their bigger bodies and electrical lures – the glowing balls of skin that hung down from their foreheads – were strong enough to get through the very tough training and pass the tests that allowed them to join the Shoal Navy.

The Shoal Navy supplied all Hydron's soldiers, and all the police for its cities. Every Assembly guard was a low swimmer. The low swimmers had been doing the same jobs for hundreds of years. They had their own traditions of celebrating ancient battles and honours won.

Their history was something that the highest-ranking officer in the Shoal Navy was very proud of. His name was Admiral Icktheus, and he was one of the largest low swimmers in the oceans of Hydron. His office was in the basement of the low swimmers' building, where there was almost no light. Since low swimmers had evolved at greater depths than the other members of the Shoal, they preferred it dark.

At this precise moment, Admiral Icktheus was floating in his office behind a stone desk. He was wearing what looked like sunglasses. The darkened lenses shielded his bulging golden eyes from the tiny amount of light that came in through the gaps in the coral branches. Admiral Icktheus hated the light. He wished he could live in the deeper pools of the ocean, but because he was so important he had to be in the capital city.

Admiral Icktheus was in charge of the safety and defence of the Shoal. He had been told about the aliens and their vessel as soon as Makron mentioned it to Darkin. There had been a meeting of the Assembly, and Icktheus said they should destroy the invaders right away. The governors did not like that idea; they wanted to see if the visitors were friendly first.

Icktheus had shaken his head slowly. They were mad, he said. They knew that these humans were there to hurt them. Why did they pretend this was not the case?

But his plan had not been accepted. They told him he needed to come up with a new idea. So he chose one very good soldier to go on board the craft and give the humans a virus.

He wanted the virus to be deadly. He wanted to wipe out the humans on the ship. But, again, the governors refused him. Instead, they just wanted to make the humans sick, not kill them. But Icktheus already knew humans, so he sent his low swimmer with a 'friendly' yellow virus.

However, making the humans ill had not slowed them down. Icktheus was shocked to discover that the craft was still heading for one of the Founts. Shock had turned to anger when he realised which Fount they were trying to reach.

Without first checking with the Assembly, the admiral had ordered his marine commandos to stop the humans' ship. He knew that the governors would be weak; he knew they would ask him not to hurt the humans, so he had told his soldiers not to hurt them. For the moment, anyway.

Now he was waiting for an update on how that attack had gone. He hoped it had been successful. He reached into a small cage on his desk and pulled out a little creature that looked like a sea snail. He popped it into his mouth and chewed it with a revolting crunching sound. Ooze from the snail's body dribbled down his chin, and he wiped it away with a thick fin on his flipper.

One of his junior officers appeared at the curtain of seaweed that hung over his office door. The officer pulsed the colour turquoise. *May I come in, sir?* he asked.

A white flash from Icktheus told the young Shoaly he could enter. The smaller fish darted inside and knelt on his front and back flippers. Then he stood up and began his report.

The vessel had been attacked as the admiral had ordered. The engines had been knocked out, forcing the humans to take their strange ship to the surface for air. Icktheus smiled at this, glowing yellow with satisfaction. The young officer hesitated.

*What?* demanded the admiral. Something had gone wrong.

The low-swimmer attack squad had used a power-drain creature called a Black-Trout on the ship, and the humans had been forced to surface. However, they had a back-up engine. The Black-Trout did not work on this new engine because the power source the motor used was not the same.

*Are you telling me they use two types of fuel?* Admiral Icktheus asked.

*Yes, sir.*

*And?*

Again the officer hesitated. *The humans' ship has reached the Fount, sir.*

The admiral made a growling noise. This shocked the other Shoaly. Icktheus managed to control his temper. *What are the humans doing now?* he asked.

*We think they are trying to get to the spawning pool, sir.*

This time Admiral Icktheus could not control himself. He burst out from behind his desk, glowing red all over. He came face-to-face with the young Shoaly and slowly took off his glasses.

*Summon my personal squadron. I will deal with this myself.*

The *Ocean Explorer* was nestled in the shadow of the huge mountain. Thick cables attached to the submarine had been tied to metal loops hammered into the rock of the island's steep sides. A gangway had been set up between the side hatch in the submarine's tower and the cliff-like side of the island.

On the deck of the sub, two crew members in blue overalls were attaching ropes to the end of a special climbing gun. It looked like a harpoon gun and had a big spike sticking out of it. According to Captain Clancy, using this gun would make the climb much quicker.

The gun would shoot the great big spike into the rock as high as it could reach. Then a winch would pull one climber at a time up to where the spike was. Since the winch was fast, they would be able to climb several hundred metres in less than an hour.

In contrast, if they had started out from sea level without the gun, it would have taken them over two days to climb the island.

Rory lifted his head to gaze up at the mountain soaring over his head. Was he really going to climb this thing? He was now dressed in blue overalls, which were fitted with a climbing harness. This climbing harness reminded Rory of a strange pair of Y-front pants.

Captain Clancy came to stand beside him. 'It's easy, really,' she said.

'Really?' Rory asked. He wasn't so sure.

The last member of the ascent team joined them. He was their leader because he was the most experienced climber.

'Ready?' asked Mr Fleming.

'As I'll ever be,' Rory replied.

'Let's do this!' said the captain.

The last member of the [illegible] passed them.
He was [illegible] because he was the [illegible]
[illegible] dubbed.

'Ready?' asked Mr Fleming.

'[illegible],' Kay replied.

'Let's do this,' said the captain.

# Chapter 10

# The Stagnant Pool

The Doctor stood with his hands clasped behind his back. Amy was amazed. He'd done it. He was actually talking to the Shoal, and they were talking back to him, and everyone seemed to understand each other. Except for Amy. She sort of understood what was going on and had learnt vaguely what the colours meant, but every colour seemed to have a hundred meanings and the Doctor was doing a brilliant job of working out which one applied.

A whole group of the Shoal that looked like lion fish were now gathered in the room on the other side of the oval window, and two colourful fish were holding the Doctor's and Amy's diving suits.

'Are they letting us go?' Amy asked.

'Not exactly,' the Doctor said. 'It seems they want to show us their city. I think they want me to speak to their government or committee or assembly. I haven't quite worked out which word is the best translation.'

'You're going to speak to their leaders with a nursery-school activity pack?' Amy asked, pointing at the row of shells with coloured water in them.

'Obviously we can't take that with us,' the Doctor said. 'I have asked for some bits and bobs so I can make a portable translator. I imagine it will look a bit like a Christmas decoration, but it'll come in handy when we get a tree next year.'

They looked at one another. After the last Christmas adventure they'd had, Amy hoped that having a tree in the TARDIS would be a simple way of staying out of trouble. But she doubted it.

'So now what? Who are the bright fish people?'

The Doctor pursed his lips. 'They are medium swimmers. They're the general workforce. The guards are low swimmers. The military, basically. The stripy fellows are the high swimmers. They're in charge.'

'High rollers, more like,' Amy said.

'Well. Exactly. But please try to remember: they're Shoal, not "fish people".'

'Right,' Amy said. 'Totally different.'

'Actually they are. Very different,' the Doctor replied. 'The fish people lived in Atlantis and they looked more like people than fish.'

Amy looked at him. Then she shook her head. 'Anyway . . .'

'The leader of the Shoal is this one here. I think his name sounds like *darkness*, but I'm not sure.' The Doctor frowned at his lack of knowledge. 'He says we will be taken to a place where I can make a translation machine.'

'And then we get the grand tour?'

'Yes,' the Doctor said with a smile. 'I'm rather looking forward to that. It's been a while since I saw an underwater city.'

Fleming gave a whoop of joy – he had clearly crested the mountaintop. Rory smiled, glad to know that he and Captain Clancy were not far behind. The gun had managed to shoot the winch almost to the summit of the mountain, and it had been relatively simple for Fleming, Captain Clancy and Rory to hoist themselves up in turn to the place where the big metal spike had driven itself into the rock. From there, it was just a short scramble to the very top.

Rory sped up and emerged through the mist into bright sunshine. He scrambled over the edge of the cliff, then turned to help Captain Clancy over too. She smiled at him as he pulled her on to the summit. They stood up and joined Mr Fleming, who was staring at the view before them.

Just like the captain had said, the water volcano had a lake in a crater on the top of it. It had a thin rim, upon which the three of them were now standing, that sloped to the water's edge. The sky seemed less purple at this height – more mauve or violet than the deep purple it appeared on the surface.

*Of course*, Rory realised. Just like on Earth, the water on Hydron wasn't the same colour as the sky; it just reflected the colour of the sky above. Since the sky was purple, the ocean looked purple too.

Rory had imagined that the crater lake would be beautiful and crystal clear. After all, it was supposed to be pure water, wasn't it? However, it was anything but. In contrast to the ocean, the lake water was a dark brown colour and had an oily film on its surface. Rory wrinkled his nose. There was an unpleasant smell, like mouldy socks – and it seemed familiar.

'I wouldn't exactly tell my friends to come here on holiday,' Rory said.

'Nor would I,' the captain replied. She took off her helmet and walked towards the lake. 'What could possibly be in here that can power our reactor engines?' she asked.

'The report said that there were power readings in the water,' Fleming said. Rory thought he sounded like a bad actor who had forgotten to learn his lines and was making them up as he went along. 'Perhaps some form of mineral? Uranium? I don't know . . .'

Rory stepped towards the stagnant pool and stared down into its depths. It was only then that he started to see the shapes in the water, but because it was dark – and thick with some nasty substance – he couldn't quite make out what the shapes were.

'Have you got a torch or something we can put in the water to see what those are?' he asked.

Fleming unhooked something from his belt and handed it to Rory. 'It's a diver's flashlight,' he said.

'Thanks.' Rory took the torch, turned it on and held it under the water. Suddenly he stumbled back. He now realised why he recognised the smell – it was the same one he'd smelt in the lab on the submarine.

'No,' he said. 'It can't be.'

'What?' Fleming was by his side in an instant, a deep frown on his face.

'They're fish roe,' Rory said. 'Fish eggs! Well, the pods of the fish eggs, anyway. The same as the one you've been hiding in that secret room – the same as the one in the box!'

Fleming glared at Rory, then glanced at Captain Clancy. She pulled her gaze away from the water and looked at her security officer.

'What does he mean?' she asked. 'What fish eggs? What secret room?' Her voice was becoming louder. 'Explain yourself, Mr Fleming!' she shouted.

Fleming shook his head and slowly pulled his gun from its holster. 'Sorry, captain,' he said, 'but you don't know the whole story.'

# Chapter 11

# The Low Swimmers Take Over

The undersea cave was huge. Admiral Icktheus stood in front of a dozen rows of his best commandos. There were over a hundred low swimmers, all in full battle kit. Each had squid grenades hanging from their belts along with their forked electric weapons. Some teams had the Black-Trouts, which looked like slugs but were the size of elephants.

Icktheus was so angry about the humans that he had decided he was going to stop them once and for all. They were going to the Fount, and that was somewhere they should not be going. It was against the law – not to mention against everything the Shoal believed in – for anyone but a Shoaly to visit the Founts.

This was the force that Icktheus was going to use to try to sink the human vessel – just like he'd done with the last one, the one that had come before and caused all that trouble. Only this time he was going to succeed. And he would kill all the humans.

He was about to issue the order when one of his most trusted spies arrived. Icktheus could see him talking with one of the guards at the cave entrance. Since Icktheus had given the order that no one was to be allowed in, the guards weren't going to let the spy pass. The admiral tore himself away from the troops and swam quickly to the cave entrance. He dismissed the guards and watched as the spy delivered his message.

*I have learnt something unbelievable*, the spy said. *Some time ago, a group of low swimmers caught a small craft with two humans aboard.*

The stripes on Admiral Icktheus's face slowly turned from their usual grey to a deep red. *Why wasn't I told about this?*

*The low swimmers who caught them have been kept in the rooms by the Assembly members*, the spy reported calmly. *Apparently they feared that you would react badly* . . .

*And they were right!* Icktheus could not help himself. The growl came from deep in his throat and built to a roar that echoed through the water. Even his hardened troops stared in shock at the admiral.

*I cannot allow this to happen*, he said. *We have a proud tradition of defending our people from any and all threats! And now we are imprisoned and kept quiet because they do not want us to do our job properly?*

He turned and swam back to the waiting commandos.

*First two squads, come with me now! There are aliens in the city!*

The Doctor and Amy were once again wearing the orange diving suits from the *Verne*. The Shoal had returned them, and Amy and the Doctor had quickly put them on.

'The leader says we're going to a laboratory,' the Doctor explained. 'Once we go out into the corridor, they'll flood the place again and then we can swim.'

They were led into the corridor and the cell door closed. Water flooded in through pipes in the wall until the passage was completely submerged. Another door opened and they were ushered through.

The Doctor activated his radio and spoke to Amy. 'I think this is some sort of military or police building.'

'Why do you think that?'

'Well, you don't find cells in normal houses, do you? Well, not most normal houses.'

Amy nodded. She had to agree with that.

After swimming down two more corridors, they entered a large room that was full of strange equipment and tools.

'Brilliant!' the Doctor said. 'Look at all this stuff. I love stuff. You can do all sorts of stuff with stuff.'

He quickly set about building what Amy thought of as his flashy light communicator thing. It had a rainbow of lights on it as well as a camera and a microcomputer, a speaker and a microphone.

'I've programmed the computer with what I've learnt from our coloured water experiments,' the Doctor explained. 'The translator will film the Shoal and translate via the speaker unit. We can then talk to them by speaking into the microphone and the machine will flash the correct lights so the Shoal can understand us.'

The Doctor told the guards that he had finished, and the Shoal leader arrived. He flashed in various colours and the translator relayed his words back to Amy and the Doctor in English.

'We are going to address the Assembly,' he said. 'Please come with me. We will be travelling through our capital city, Reef.'

Inside his diving helmet, Amy could see the Doctor grinning.

They swam to an exit, where there was a large grey creature resting on the seabed. It looked like some kind of whale. Amy was quite alarmed when it opened its massive mouth and two of the Shoal swam inside and rested against the creature's teeth, standing on what she guessed was its tongue. Amy pulled a face and stepped back. Not so the Doctor – he stepped straight up and climbed inside.

At first Amy was not at all keen to get inside the whale. Not after the last one! She shivered as she remembered *Starship UK* and being in the belly of the Star Whale. She knew that you didn't escape without a lot of fuss and probably some whale sick . . .

The amazing thing was that, although the whale looked grey from outside, once inside it was possible to see through its skin, sort of like tinted glass windows in a car. The giant fish rose from the sand and started swimming. Two low swimmers in what looked like metal armour swam alongside the whale. Amy was reminded of the President of the United States' limo driving through the streets with a police motorcycle escort.

As the whale made its way through the city, Amy looked out through its transparent skin. She thought that Reef was beautiful. There was so much colour and life here. It was like Piccadilly Circus in London, or Times Square in New York. There were so many creatures going about their lives, and the view of the seaweed and coral was mind-blowing. She could see why the Doctor had smiled at the thought of exploring this place; she couldn't help doing the same.

The Doctor was chatting to the Shoal's leader. His machine translated whatever he said into the flashing lights, but she guessed the Doctor had already picked up the Shoal language so he could understand what they were saying anyway. It was a bit like listening to a friend on a mobile phone.

He had managed to work out the Shoal's individual names, too. He leaned over to Amy. 'The leader of the Shoal is called Darkin, and the younger Shoaly is his son. His name is Makron.'

Finally they slowed down, as the whale approached a large round orange building with seaweed all over its roof.

'So that's your Assembly building?' the Doctor asked. 'Look, Amy!'

It looked like a pineapple to Amy. A pineapple under the sea! She laughed. 'SpongeBob!' she said.

The Doctor frowned. 'What are you talking about, Pond?'

Amy shook her head. 'Never mind.' Then she realised that she might have been a bit rude to the Shoal. 'It looks very nice.' She smiled warmly at

Makron, whose skin flushed a light pink colour. Perhaps he was blushing? Amy doubted it.

The whale creature came to a stop in a large alcove below the Assembly building. Amy swam out of the whale's mouth and straight into the building's orange corridors. The Doctor followed her, along with Darkin and Makron. The guards had vanished, but Amy supposed they must trust her and the Doctor now, thanks to the Doctor's eagerness to communicate with them.

As they emerged into a bigger entrance hall, the ugliest fish Amy had ever seen swam up to them, surrounded by twenty more low swimmers. They all had their forked weapons out and were not just pointing them at Amy and the Doctor but also at Makron and Darkin.

The Doctor grimaced as the ugly fish and Darkin pulsed and flashed at each other. He turned to Amy and whispered, 'Oh dear. I don't think this will end well. This chap's an admiral and he is saying that the Assembly has betrayed him. That we are aliens and that we are dangerous.'

'Well that's not true!' Amy said.

This attracted the attention of Admiral Ugly. He swam right up to her and touched her diving helmet with his glowing green lure. There was a sizzle of electricity and Amy felt that the world was swimming – not her. She watched in a daze as the Doctor stepped up to the big fish and started talking to him very loudly.

Then she fainted and the world went black.

# Chapter 12
# The Secret of the Shoal

Rory looked at the gun Fleming was holding. Was he serious? Rory had never really liked the man, but what was he doing? Rory didn't understand, and it seemed Captain Clancy didn't either.

'So tell me! What is going on here?' she shouted.

Fleming smiled. 'You were told that we've never been to this planet before, weren't you?'

'Yes.' Clancy looked confused.

'That's not true,' Fleming said. 'I have been to this planet before. I came here two years ago with another team.' He stopped smiling. 'Things went wrong.'

Rory looked at the security officer and suddenly he knew what had happened. 'You came here and you took some of those creatures' eggs, and now they're angry. That's why they're attacking us.'

'We . . . we didn't know they were intelligent,' Fleming said. 'At first we just thought they were just fish.' He paused. 'They *are* fish! Now, get on the radio, captain. We need to haul a pump up here with a pipe long enough to reach back to the sub.'

'But why steal their eggs – their children?' Clancy looked at Fleming. She had tears in her eyes.

Rory felt both angry and sick at the same time.

'For what the eggs are made of,' Fleming said. 'When they decompose they create amazing amounts of power. I've never seen anything like it. We tested them aboard the old submarine. The *Marine Adventurer*, it was called.' He laughed bitterly. 'Some adventure. Everyone died. Except for me and Angela Morton, that is.'

'But we don't need any more power,' Clancy said. 'We've got all sorts of fuel. We don't need this.' She waved a hand at the polluted lake.

'You don't understand,' Fleming said. 'Just one of these things could power a starship for a week. It would make anyone a fortune.'

'So you poisoned the water here?' asked Rory through gritted teeth. 'This is where those fish grow up. This is their nursery.'

Fleming pointed his gun at Rory. 'Stay back, nurse!' he said. Then he turned to Clancy. 'I said get on the radio, captain. Do it!'

Clancy wasn't left with much choice: she radioed the *Ocean Explorer.*

Amy awoke to find that she was back on the floor of the cell. She was still wearing the orange diving suit, but her helmet was gone. She lifted her head and looked around the now-familiar cell. The Doctor was standing by the door. Amy could just see a low swimmer through the glass window.

'What happened?' she asked.

'The admiral took a dislike to you,' the Doctor said, coming over to squat next to Amy. He placed his hand gently on her forehead, then pulled down the eyelid on her left eye and stared at her eye. Finally he stuck his tongue out. Amy did the same.

'Good.' The Doctor stood up.

'Admiral?' asked Amy. 'What did he do, though?'

'He stunned you with his lure – that special type of fin that sticks out from a low swimmer's head.'

'The green, glowing thing?'

The Doctor nodded. 'And he's an admiral, yes. Admiral Icktheus: the most senior officer in the Shoal's Navy. He's taken over. We're all prisoners. Me, you,

Darkin and most of the other governors, too. Makron managed to get away.'

'After all our work? We'll never get away now!'

'We will get away. We must.' The Doctor lowered his voice. 'If we don't, the admiral is going to execute us.'

'If he wants us dead, why are we in a cell?' Amy was angry now.

'He wants a public execution – he wants to show everyone that we are bad aliens and that he is doing a good job.'

'And I presume your coloured-light machine won't get us out of this?'

'I think not,' the Doctor whispered. 'But I do still have this!' He held the sonic screwdriver up to Amy in his right hand.

'Great. So what are we waiting for? Let's get out of here!' She stood up and crossed to the door.

'It's not that easy,' the Doctor said. 'There is a large low swimmer out there armed with a very nasty-looking fork.'

As he spoke, the very large low swimmer suddenly fell back against the window and slid down it until his head vanished from view. A few seconds later, Makron's face appeared. He was waving his own pronged weapon and had the Doctor's translation device in his other fin.

The Doctor grinned and immediately pointed the sonic screwdriver at the door. After a few seconds' buzzing, the lock clicked open. The Doctor and Amy hurried out of the cell, stepping over the sleeping body of the low swimmer. Makron passed the translator to the Doctor and they quickly started talking.

'You need to come with me. Now!' Makron said via the translator.

They ran down the short corridor in the opposite direction they had taken earlier. Another low swimmer was lying on the floor; Amy guessed Makron must have already knocked him out. Set into the wall was a stone door. The Shoaly pressed a button, and it slid back to reveal what looked like a cupboard. Then Amy saw that there was another door opposite her.

'What's this?' she asked.

'Waterlock,' the Doctor replied. He took her arm and guided her inside the small chamber. 'Like an airlock, but for water.'

Amy looked at him and shrugged. 'What does that mean?'

Makron had now joined them in the tiny room and the first door was closing.

'It means that when that door closes the chamber will fill with water,' Makron said via the translator.

'Then the second door will open and we'll be able to swim out.'

'But we haven't got our helmets! We'll drown,' exclaimed Amy. Then she squealed as she noticed that water was already lapping at her ankles and rising fast.

'Don't worry!' the Doctor said, pinching his nose. 'Just hold your breath!'

Before Amy could ask another question, the water level had reached her neck. She took a huge gulp of air just before the water rose over her head and filled the room. The second door opened.

Looking through water without goggles is a bit like looking at a photo that is out of focus. Everything was hazy, but Amy could definitely see that beyond the door was a larger area with a line of bright lights set into the walls. They were all shining on a big yellow object floating in the middle of the space.

The Doctor tugged at her sleeve and they started swimming towards the large yellow blob. As they got nearer, Amy realised that it was the *Verne*, the little submersible they had taken from the *Ocean Explorer*. The Doctor helped her into the airlock on top of the sub and closed the hatch on her. Amy was now bursting to breathe. Her cheeks were puffed out and she needed air urgently. Just when she thought she couldn't bear it any more, the water in the airlock was sucked away and she gasped in big lungfuls of air.

Then she remembered that the Doctor was waiting in the water. Quickly she undid the lock on the inner door and climbed down into the *Verne*'s cockpit. Her diving suit was full of water but she ignored the discomfort. Instead, she slammed the hatch shut and spun the handle that locked it.

Amy listened as the Doctor opened the outer hatch with a dull thud. This was followed by another thud as he closed it, then a hissing sound as the airlock drained the water away. The handle on the inner hatch turned and the Doctor climbed down.

He looked fine. Amy was still breathing hard, grateful for the oxygen. The Doctor simply looked like he'd come in out of a heavy rain shower. He smiled and closed the little round door again.

'Can we get out of here now?' Amy slumped into one of the pilot's chairs.

'Don't forget about Makron.' They waited for the airlock to go through its process once more, then the Shoaly got into the small cockpit with them. It was quite cramped, but the three of them managed to get arranged comfortably, with the Doctor and Amy in the pilots' seats and Makron crouched behind them.

'Hang on,' said Amy. 'Fish – sorry, Shoaly. How do you survive out of water? I thought that sea creatures died out of water?'

'Most do,' Makron said, through the translation device. 'We are more advanced than most fish. We can live in air for several hours.'

'Very useful,' the Doctor said. 'Now let's go!'

He pressed the start button on the control panel. The *Verne* gave a small jerk, then motored away from the brightly lit area and down a dark tunnel.

## Chapter 13

# The *Verne* Escapes

The pump at the top of the water volcano was making a noise like a dentist's suction tube. Fleming had forced Captain Clancy and Rory to lower two thick cables from the cliff's edge down to the submarine below. Then the security officer had made them pull the lines back up. It was very hard work and they were both sweating a lot by the time the equipment appeared over the rim of the crater.

Fleming set up the machinery while Clancy and Rory lowered the cables again, this time to bring up the thick pipe that would take the discarded egg sacks down to the engines of the *Ocean Explorer.*

'What are you going to do when you've refuelled the sub?' asked Rory.

'Be quiet,' Fleming spat. His attention was fixed on the pump, and he was making sure that it was working properly. 'We don't need much,' he called to Clancy. Then he stood up and walked to the cliff's edge. He peered down into the misty cloud.

'They're pretty powerful. Like I said, one egg pod can power a spaceship. But these have been lying around for ages. We'll have to see what we can get out of them. Before that, we need to get back down.'

Fleming stood back from the edge, then turned round. 'Now that we've finished using the winch to bring stuff up, we can use it to send things down,' he said, grabbing Rory by the shoulders and securing the end of the cable that was connected to the winch to Rory's climbing harness. He then yanked Rory to the edge of the crater.

'Unfortunately, I need you,' Fleming said. 'I'd happily leave you up here but you're the only one who can make Angela better. So you've got to come back down.'

Rory peered over the side. It certainly was a very long way down. He looked back and saw that although the cable was attached to the winch, there was a loose pile of cable that hadn't been fed back on the machine.

'Hang on,' Rory said. 'You need to –'

'We need to get down in a hurry,' Fleming whispered in his ear. 'You'd better hope the cable is strong enough to take the strain.'

Rory opened his mouth to argue, but Fleming put one large hand in the middle of his back and pushed. Rory found himself falling through the air, the cable streaming out above him.

He screamed as he fell.

Makron helped guide the Doctor and Amy through the secret tunnel and out into the open sea beyond Reef. While Amy enjoyed the new sights and the different beings she met while travelling with the Doctor, she was glad they were now heading back to the *Ocean Explorer*.

'What do you think's been happening on the sub?' Amy asked.

'I'm not sure,' the Doctor said. He was concentrating on the *Verne*'s controls.

'Rory's probably been having a whale of a time!' she joked.

The Doctor looked up. 'What?' he asked. 'Oh yes. Whale. Very good, Pond!'

One of the instruments on the control panel began to buzz.

'It's a signal,' the Doctor said. 'It's very weak, but it might be the submarine!'

He set the engines to go as fast as they could. As they sped along, the Doctor asked Makron about his people.

'Tell me, Makron, how do your people work with electricity underwater? Usually the two don't mix very well.'

The translator flashed and the computer voice said, 'You humans have blood running through your veins. The Shoal have blood, but we also have electricity in our bodies. Almost all sea creatures on Hydron do.'

'So it's a natural thing?' Amy asked.

'Yes. We can feed on it and use it before we even hatch from our eggs.'

'So the Shoal lay eggs?' the Doctor said. 'Of course you do. Sorry.'

'Like a chicken!' Amy said.

The Doctor shushed her. 'Chicken's eggs have a yolk which is full of food for the baby chick to feed on. Shoaly eggs don't have a yolk. Instead they have some form of electrical charge stored in the roe somehow.'

'We need very large amounts of energy to survive while we are in our eggs.'

'And that's how the low swimmers can electrocute people with their lures?'

'That's right,' Makron said. 'The low swimmers can focus the electricity in their lures and use it as a weapon, but the high and medium swimmers can only use it to power torches or other items that need electricity when we touch them.

'Once a year, all members of the Shoal who want to have children swim to the spawning grounds,' Makron went on. 'There are many Founts on Hydron, but different ones are used each year depending on the moons and the tides.'

While they were talking, the *Verne* was homing in on the signal the Doctor had picked up as they left Reef. Now a red warning light began to flash on the control panel, telling them they were getting closer to whatever was sending the signal.

While the Doctor attended to the controls, Amy continued the conversation to find out all she could about the Shoal.

'What's a Fount?' she asked.

'A Fount is an amazing sea mountain,' Makron told her. 'It rises into the air as high as the sea is deep. At the top are pools of the purest fresh water.'

The Doctor's hands flowed across the controls as if he had been driving submersibles his whole life. He turned back to Makron. 'Your whole culture is based on electricity, even though you live underwater!' the Doctor said. 'And how quickly do the Shoal grow once the eggs have been laid?'

'We hatch in a matter of days,' Makron said. 'We are almost fully grown when we hatch. We can swim and eat normally. We don't need the electricity to feed upon any more. But we have changed from needing fresh water to live in to needing salt water.'

'Aha!' the Doctor said. 'Just like salmon on Earth. They swim upriver from the sea to lay their eggs.' He chuckled. 'This mad old universe!'

'We have to leave the Founts as soon as we can, otherwise we'll die. We have to go down the Drops.'

Before Amy could ask what the Drops were, the buzzing on the control panel became a bleeping. The Doctor had brought the submersible to the surface of the ocean, and gentle waves lapped at the viewscreen in front of the pilots' seats. Twenty metres away a small grey object smaller than the *Verne* floated in the water.

'What's that?' Amy asked. It certainly wasn't the *Ocean Explorer.*

'I would say it is an emergency buoy of some kind,' the Doctor said. 'They probably launched it when we went missing. I wonder why they didn't wait for us?'

Makron flashed turquoise and green. 'They were attacked by the low swimmers,' the machine translated.

'What?' Amy looked shocked.

'My father gave Admiral Icktheus permission to give the crew aboard the *Ocean Explorer* a virus,' Makron explained.

The Doctor did not look pleased. 'Why did he do that?' he asked.

'Because the last time there was a human ship here, they attacked us. They stole our children!' Makron flashed an angry red.

'Tell me what happened,' the Doctor said. 'I want to know everything.'

## Chapter 14

# Makron's Story

The Doctor and Amy sat and listened as Makron told them what had happened the last time that humans had come to his planet.

'Several seasons ago visitors came to my planet,' Makron said. 'We weren't stupid enough to think that we were the only living things in the galaxy, but it was a bit of a shock. Everything about the aliens surprised us.'

'First contact with another species is always difficult,' the Doctor said, and Amy nodded. Look at what had happened between the humans and Silurians on Earth!

'They looked different to us and they had big machines that they used for travelling underwater,' Makron went on. 'At first we called them the Hurry, because they all wore orange when they were outside their ship. We thought that these creatures had orange skin! We had no idea that they needed clothes to swim under the water and that, in fact, each one was a slightly different colour of white or pink or brown.'

'Hurry is a good word for humans,' the Doctor said. 'Always rushing into things.'

'The most surprising thing about them was that they didn't even notice us. Our scientists had seen their ship above our planet even before they dropped an underwater travel machine into the sea.'

'A submarine,' Amy clarified.

'Is that what they call it?' asked Makron. 'Well, we learnt about this submarine and we were very curious. We wanted to know who these aliens were and what they were looking for. But we were also scared. We decided to watch first, to see what these new people might be like.'

'So you followed the submarine?' the Doctor asked.

Makron nodded. 'Yes. They were exploring and we were worried. They had arrived during spawning season. A lot of Shoaly were making their way to the Founts. The movement of so many large creatures couldn't be hidden, and the humans noticed and followed the Shoaly.'

'I bet Admiral Icktheus was very cross,' Amy said. 'He seems the type!'

'My father wanted us to go to the humans and tell them that the Founts were sacred. Only adult Shoaly can go there, and then they only get to go once in their lifetimes. It's a really special time of year. We have feasts and there are fun things to do.'

'Sort of like Christmas,' Amy said. She was shocked by Makron's story. She thought this sort of thing just didn't happen any more.

'Exactly,' the Doctor replied. 'Then what happened?'

'Icktheus convinced the Assembly that they should attack the humans to show them that they were doing something wrong. There was a battle between the low swimmers and the humans.' Makron paused. His mouth opened and closed several times as if he was uncomfortable.

The Doctor bowed his head. 'I am sorry if this is difficult,' he said.

Makron's eyes closed. 'The humans did something terrible,' he said. 'I don't know how they did it but they poisoned the water of the Fount. The whole Assembly wanted the humans dead then. So the low swimmers attacked the submarine.'

'And it sank,' the Doctor said. 'Was everyone aboard killed?'

'There was no one on board,' Makron said, opening his eyes again. 'They had all gone to the

Fount. Not long after that, the spaceship took the surviving humans away and we never saw them again – until now.'

'I was right.' The Doctor sighed. 'The humans were hiding something. I don't know if Captain Clancy is involved, but Mr Fleming definitely knows about this previous mission. The question is, just how much does he know?'

# Chapter 15
# The Wreck

The Doctor sat back in the pilot's chair, shaking his head. Amy wiped a tear from her cheek. Makron looked sad.

'Both sides are at fault,' the Doctor said. 'However, the humans' lack of respect for your planet and people is worse than your desire to defend yourselves.'

He turned back to the controls and started getting the submersible ready to dive.

'Where are we going?' Amy asked.

'We need to stop this becoming a full-scale war,' the Doctor said. 'The Shoal – or at least Admiral Icktheus and his low swimmers – are following the *Ocean Explorer*. If they manage to catch up with the submarine before we do, they will sink it and kill everyone on board.'

He set the final controls and pushed the square steering wheel forward, angling the submersible downward. There was a grim expression on his face that Amy recognised as determination.

'But what can we do in this little thing?' Amy made a circle in the air with her finger to indicate the *Verne*'s tiny interior.

'Don't worry about that,' the Doctor replied. His mouth was showing a hint of a smile now. 'I have a plan . . .'

The refuelling was complete and the *Ocean Explorer* was already miles away from the polluted Fount. Rory was back in the medical bay looking after the sick crew members, although now he had one of Mr Fleming's armed security guards standing over him all the time.

He had hated being pushed from the clifftop. The fall must have taken only a few seconds but it had seemed to Rory to take forever. Just when he had thought he was going to faint from fear, the cable had snapped tight and he had bounced up again. He supposed it was a bit like an unplanned bungee jump.

It had only taken half an hour for the winch to lower him the few thousand feet to the submarine below. All that time Rory had been thinking. He was wondering how the Doctor and Amy were doing and where they could be. He hoped he would see them again soon. He missed Amy, but he knew she was safe with the Doctor.

He also thought about Mr Fleming and why he wanted to take the fish creatures' egg cases. He knew it was for money, but he was shocked at how some people would do anything to be rich. Rory would always rather have a clear conscience than a lot of money. He couldn't live with himself if he did something as bad as Fleming had.

Captain Clancy and Fleming had followed him down. Before they all returned to the submarine, Fleming had threatened to kill both Rory and Clancy – as well as the rest of the crew – if Clancy didn't do exactly what Fleming wanted.

Fleming forced Rory down the ladder into the control room, where two more security guards stood with their guns held at the ready.

'This man is under arrest,' Fleming said. 'Take him to the medical bay and watch him. If he does anything suspicious, shoot him.'

Rory was pushed down the submarine's corridors at gunpoint and eventually reached the medical bay. Here, the guard stood outside the door with his gun held tightly across his chest.

'Welcome back,' said MARVE.

'Hello, MARVE,' Rory replied. 'Did you miss me?'

'No.' The robot's two camera eyes looked at Rory without emotion. Then the screen under the eyes showed a smile. 'Just kidding!'

'Ha ha,' said Rory. 'So, what's new?'

'There has been a mutiny and Mr Fleming's guards have taken over the submarine.'

Rory looked at the robot. 'Yeah,' he said. 'Thanks for that.' He sank down into one of the plastic chairs by the table.

At the front of the *Ocean Explorer*, Captain Jane Clancy was sitting in a chair that belonged to one of the control-room crew members. Fleming was sitting in the captain's command chair, and she didn't like that.

The moment the submarine had dived underwater again, Fleming had ordered one of the eggs to be brought to the control room. Now it sat next to him, bobbing in its glass tube and pressing itself against the side of its container like a child staring through a toy-shop window.

'Why is it doing that?' asked Clancy.

Fleming looked over at her. 'The eggs like being in a group, so each one will always point towards the largest number of other eggs nearby.'

'You're using it as a tracker?'

'You saw the lake. It was stagnant, dead. They must be using a new water-filled volcano and this thing will tell me how to find it.'

Clancy sighed. 'So that's why you needed the eggs *on board*.'

She shook her head. She was powerless. There was nothing she could do to stop this madman – but she could at least try to find out the whole story.

'Why wasn't I told about the other submarine?' she asked. 'Why did the company hide this from me and my crew?'

'Because I told them to,' he said.

'Why would they do what *you* told them?' Clancy frowned. Fleming stood up and came over to her. He bent down to whisper in her ear and she shuddered.

'I was the only one who came back from Hydron,' he breathed. 'I could tell them anything I liked. Who else could they ask to check that what I said was the truth?'

Clancy's eyes widened. 'You lied to them?'

'I told them that the whole expedition had been a disaster. I told them that there were people left behind on the other submarine.'

'What?' Clancy was confused.

'I wasn't going to let the company know about the fish eggs,' Fleming said. 'Not when I could come and take them for myself. So I told them that the fish creatures had attacked the submarine and we'd been forced to leave them and return to Earth.'

Clancy blinked at the madman. 'I get it,' she said. 'There's no way the company would have told anyone about that. The government would have closed them down if they did.'

'You got it,' Fleming said. 'So I suggested they mount another mission with a cover story. I told them we could say there were useful mineral deposits here. I told them that when we got here I would reveal the secret, real mission – to rescue the survivors.'

'Very clever,' Clancy said. 'All so you could get your hands on the eggs.' She shook her head, disgusted. 'And how do you plan to get away with it?'

Smiling, Fleming walked back to the captain's chair and patted the glass tube with the pod inside.

'These egg cases are going to make me rich,' he said. 'All I need to do is find them. And, when I do, I'm going to take the whole lot with me.'

'But what about the baby fish inside?'

'I'm not going to wait for them to hatch!' Fleming laughed. 'In case you've forgotten, we've got a whole ocean of fish creatures after us. We won't have time to stop.'

'But the baby fish . . .' Clancy gasped. 'They'll be killed.'

'So what?' Fleming's eyes became misty, as if he was imagining himself rolling in money. 'Last time we only managed to get five. This time we'll get the whole lake full! Thousands of them. *Thousands!*'

The small yellow submersible moved slowly through the dark waters at the base of the undersea cliffs. The various lights on its hull shone into the gloom, picking out the volcanic rocks and the nervous creatures that lived there.

Inside the cockpit, a steady beeping told the three passengers that the sub was dangerously close to the ocean floor and in danger of crashing into it. The Doctor ignored the sound and concentrated instead on the controls.

He was gently steering the *Verne* towards something that the sonar showed up as a large bump on the seabed. A readout on the control panel displayed how close they were to 'contact'.

Amy looked at the digital green display. It read: 8.73 METRES. Everyone was holding their breath. Even the Doctor was biting his lip.

Makron leaned forward and flashed a question. 'Will we be able to get on board?'

The Doctor didn't answer at first. He was still concentrating. The green numbers flicked down and down: 5.68 METRES . . . 5.03 METRES . . .

'If it looks okay . . .' The Doctor moved the position of the outside light. Suddenly a huge grey figure filled the screens. 'There she is!' he laughed and clapped his hands.

Amy couldn't help smiling too.

The *Verne* moved forward over the sunken wreck of a submarine. It was the *Marine Adventurer*, the sub that the Shoal had sunk when the humans had last visited Hydron.

'She's still airtight,' the Doctor said, reading a computer screen.

'What does that mean?' asked Amy.

'It means that the submarine might still be working!'

Chapter 16

# The Doctor to the Rescue!

Rory was hunched over a microscope, peering down at the image of the virus. Unable to do anything to escape, Rory had decided to double-check MARVE's test results to see if there really was no cure for the virus. As far as he could tell the robot was right: they could give the patients medicines and antibiotics, but all this did was bring down their temperatures.

Suddenly he felt the deck of the submarine tilt. He looked down at his feet. The *Ocean Explorer* was surfacing! He stood up, turned and went to the door. The security guard was standing opposite him in the corridor. He looked at Rory without expression.

'What's happening?' Rory asked.

'We must have reached the next water volcano,' the guard said. 'Captain Fleming is bringing the sub up so that we can radio the drop ship.'

'Why can't you just radio underwater?'

'You can't use a radio underwater. It's like being underground. The signal can't get through. You need to have an aerial on the surface.'

Rory looked at him, then his eyebrows lowered. 'Hang on. What drop ship? Do you mean the *Cosmic Rover*?'

The guard nodded.

The *Ocean Explorer*'s periscope broke the surface of the purple sea, leaving a V-shape of bubbles behind it. Bit by bit, the tower also emerged from the water, then finally the rest of the deck rose out of the water too, ploughing through the waves. The hatch on top of the tower opened and Fleming climbed out on to the slippery metal.

He looked out over the rail to the mountain that lay ahead of the sub. It was different from the last one. The rock was a different colour – more brown than grey. He brought a pair of binoculars to his eyes for a better look and saw that there was even a more level piece of land at the edge of the sea.

It didn't matter. His plan didn't involve climbing up the cliffs – not this time. Instead, he would radio the spaceship in orbit above them. The automatic pilot would bring the ship down into the atmosphere of Hydron and it would collect the *Ocean Explorer* in its huge metal clamps. Then it would lift the sub over the top of the mountain and drop it in the freshwater lake at the summit. This might kill a few of the fish creatures, but that didn't matter to Fleming. He was going to kill them all anyway with the *Cosmic Rover*'s lasers.

Then he would be able to collect all the eggs and leave this stupid purple planet forever. He'd sell the eggs to the company and retire to Catrigan Nova with its whirlpools of gold. Easy.

Without warning, a hundred low swimmers appeared in the water about a kilometre off the starboard bow. A dozen or so larger fish accompanied the low swimmers.

Fleming lowered his binoculars. Whatever the low swimmers had planned, he didn't care. This time, he was ready for them. This time, it would be *them* sinking to the bottom of the sea.

'Have you signalled the drop ship?' he asked, speaking into his radio.

'Yes, sir,' a voice crackled back.

'Good. Then arm the torpedoes!' He jumped down through the hatch and closed the doorway above him. 'And prepare the poison!' he shouted.

He slid down the ladder and came to a halt in the control room.

'We have one hundred and twenty-four contacts, Mr Fleming,' one of the crew members reported. 'They're maintaining a distance of eight hundred metres.'

'Staying put, eh?' Fleming laughed. 'They'll be sitting targets.'

He sat down in the captain's chair and listened as the crew member reported the situation. The submarine dipped beneath the water once more.

'Contacts now three hundred metres.'

'Fire the forward torpedoes! All tubes!' bellowed Fleming.

Another crew member in black overalls pressed some buttons and six small lights on her panel lit up. 'Six tubes armed and ready,' she said.

'Wait!' Clancy shouted. She had to try one last time. 'Please don't do this. You'll be starting a war with those creatures.'

Fleming looked at her. His face was red with anger. 'How dare you challenge me?' he screamed. He jumped up from his chair and grabbed the nearest armed guard. He dragged the unfortunate crew member over to where Clancy was sitting. 'I am relieving Captain Clancy of her command. If she does that again – shoot her!'

He marched forward and stood right in front of the screens and next to the guard who had armed the torpedoes. With a brief look of defiance at Clancy, Fleming pressed in turn each of the six lights on the torpedo-control panel.

'Fire!' he hissed.

*WHOOOSH!*

The torpedoes left the nose of the submarine and disappeared into the darkness, leaving a cloud of bubbles.

*Ping.*

The sonar sounded as the sound waves reflected from the underwater missiles.

*Ping-ping-ping.*

The pings became faster as the torpedoes got closer to their targets. Fleming clenched his fist. He knew the first weapon would strike home any second.

*Ping-ping-ping-pi–*

The sonar went silent.

'What's going on?' Fleming looked down at the guard sitting at the torpedo-control panel.

'The torpedoes have been . . .' She shrugged. 'Well, they've been switched off, sir.'

'Switched off?' Fleming was about to start shouting again, but then something hit the submarine. The impact threw him forward and he hit his head on the corner of the screen. He sat down on the floor and put his hand to his head. When he took it away his fingers had blood on them.

'Get that nurse up here,' he said, looking at his hand. Then he glanced up, as if he was seeing the control room for the first time. A guard jumped forward and helped Fleming to his feet.

'What hit us?' Fleming asked.

The sonar operator hesitated.

'Well?' demanded Fleming.

'The computer says it was another submarine, sir.'

'Impossible! The fish creatures must have a device that reflects sonar images or something.' Fleming smiled. A trickle of blood ran down his forehead and caught in his eyebrow. 'But it doesn't matter what devices they have. Is the poison ready?'

'Yes, sir. The tanks have been filled with 7D-24.'

'That will kill everything closer than a hundred metres to the ship almost instantly!' Clancy interrupted, just as Rory entered the control room with his guard. He looked at Fleming and his bleeding head.

'Exactly!' Fleming turned to Clancy with a shark-like grin. Then he placed a hand on the shoulder of the crew member operating the water tanks. 'Release the poison!'

*CREEEEEEEEEEEAAAAAK . . .*

A piercing noise filled the submarine. It was a really loud, high-pitched buzzing, as if there were a million angry bees behind the sub's walls, and it set Rory's teeth on edge.

'I WOULDN'T DO THAT IF I WERE YOU!'

Everyone looked about. The voice had come from all around them.

'Who is that?' shouted Fleming.

Rory smiled, walked forward and spoke to the room as if he was talking to an invisible magic creature.

'Hello, Doctor!' he said.

'HELLO, RORY!' the voice boomed back. Rory smiled a huge smile.

'Hello, Amy!' Rory called.

'The Doctor? But he's dead,' Fleming said.

'LIKE MOST OF MY ENEMIES, YOU'VE DISCOVERED I'M A BIT DIFFICULT TO KILL!'

There was a sort of muffled sound of the Doctor talking to someone else.

The screen at the front of the control room flickered, then filled with a picture of the Doctor's face.

'Is that better?' he asked. 'Not so loud?'

'I am the captain of this submarine,' Fleming screamed at the Doctor's face.

'No, you're not,' the Doctor replied. 'Jane Clancy is.'

Jane lifted her chin and smiled.

'You have no authority here, Doctor!' Fleming yelled.

'Oh, stop shouting,' the Doctor said. 'I have every right to replace you with a frog if I want to, and don't think I'm not tempted. But Captain Jane is a good woman, and right now I need her.'

'I thought we were under attack,' Rory said.

'Ah, well, I hooked the sonic screwdriver up to this submarine's sonar system and deployed what they call a "towed array" – a whole load of microphones, basically. But I turned them into speakers. Anyway, when I switched it to maximum, it knocked out all the low swimmers.'

'But the *Verne* doesn't have a towed array,' said Clancy, standing up.

'That's because we're not on the *Verne*!' The Doctor's smile filled the screen. 'We're on the *Marine Adventurer*!'

For a moment the picture changed to that of the large grey submarine – a mirror image of its sister ship, the *Ocean Explorer*.

'That's impossible,' breathed Fleming.

Rory looked at him. 'Yeah,' he said. 'The Doctor's like that!'

The Doctor's face returned to the screen and peered at them all. 'We don't have very much time before the low swimmers wake up with nasty headaches and probably in very bad moods!' he said. Then he smiled again. 'But I'm sure we can sort everything out.'

'What do you need us to do?' asked Clancy.

'Lock *him* up for a start.' The Doctor stabbed a finger at the screen. He was pointing at Fleming.

'With pleasure,' said Captain Clancy. She marched up to Fleming, then turned to a pair of guards. 'If you know what's good for you, you will do what I say and put this man in the brig. He is no longer an officer on this ship, nor is he head of security.'

The two security guards looked at one another, then jumped forward. They each grabbed an arm and took a struggling and protesting Fleming away.

'Right,' the Doctor said. 'Don't forget that Doctor Angela Morton will also need arresting as soon as she recovers. Now! I'd like some of the crew of the *Ocean Explorer* to go with Makron here. He needs to rescue his father and the rest of the Shoal from Admiral Icktheus.' The Doctor paused. 'You won't know what

I'm talking about, but let's join the submarines and have a quick chat.'

'How do we join up the subs?' Rory asked.

'I don't know, Rory,' the Doctor said. 'Have you got any boat ties?' His smile became even wider than normal. 'Boat ties are cool!'

# Chapter 17

# The Final Mission

Half an hour later, they were all standing in the control room, preparing for their final mission. Once the submarines had surfaced, the crew had attached them together using ropes that they were now calling 'boat ties'. The Doctor and Amy had come aboard the *Ocean Explorer.* Some crew members were already with Makron and had swapped over to the *Marine Adventurer*, which was preparing to go on its rescue mission to Reef.

The Doctor sat with Amy, opposite Rory and Captain Clancy. He was explaining what they were about to do. 'We need to get up to the freshwater lake on top of the Fount – the water volcano. We need to return the eggs aboard this submarine to their rightful place.'

'Fleming has sent a message to our spaceship,' Clancy explained. 'He was going to use it to pick up the sub and drop it at the top of the mountain. It'll be here in about ninety minutes.'

'That's good,' the Doctor replied. 'We'll need to be leaving soon anyway. But we can't be dropped in the lake – that would kill any Shoaly in the way.'

The Doctor operated a control and the navigation screens flicked to reveal a diagram of the water volcano showing that the mountain was hollow. It was a bit like a basin made of stone with the lake of water at the top. The sides of the mountain came down below the level of the sea, then flattened to become the seabed.

'What's that?' Rory asked, bending forward. He pointed at a line that ran from the ocean floor right up to the bottom of the pool.

'I'm glad you asked,' the Doctor said, 'because that is where we need to take this submarine up to, so we can get the eggs back to their nursery.'

'We have to take the *Verne* up there? It looks very small,' said Captain Clancy.

Amy shook her head. 'We can't fit all the eggs in there.' She frowned. 'We have to go in this one.'

'You want to pilot the *Ocean Explorer* up through those narrow caves?' The captain shook her head. 'We can't do that. We'll never fit.'

'We have to try,' the Doctor said. 'Don't worry. I'll be here to help.' Then he leaned forward. 'One more thing.'

'Yes?'

'By the time we get going, the low swimmers will be waking up, so they'll probably be following us, trying to stop us.'

'We'd better get started then,' the captain said.

The Doctor jumped forward and kissed her cheek. 'Thank you,' he said.

Clancy blushed and then clicked on one of the navigation screens. An image of Makron appeared. He was standing next to a crew member wearing a blue uniform.

'How are we doing with the *Marine Adventurer*?' Clancy asked.

'Casting off now, ma'am,' the crew member said.

'Keep hold of that translator, Makron!' the Doctor said.

'I will,' the Shoaly replied.

'And don't forget our plan!'

'No, Doctor, I won't. As soon as I have freed my father, I'll send help.'

'We might well need it. I have a feeling that Admiral Icktheus won't be in a forgiving mood.'

Amy heard a couple of clunks as the two submarines separated once more.

'Good luck!' Makron said, glowing turquoise and yellow.

'And to you!' Amy called.

The screen went blank and the Doctor sat down in one of the sub's pilot seats.

Because there were more crew members aboard the other submarine now, the Doctor, Amy and Rory would all have to help steer and control the *Ocean Explorer.* Rory sat in one of the pilot seats, while the Doctor and Amy went over to sit at the master control panel.

'All ready?' Captain Clancy asked.

'Geroni–'

'Don't say it!' The Doctor interrupted Rory and looked at him sternly. Then he turned round and muttered, 'That's my line.'

Rory nodded. 'Oh. Okay. Um . . . yes, then!'

The captain issued her orders and the Doctor and Rory started to steer the submarine down through the sea. Amy counted off the depth at every ten metres.

As they passed 400 metres, the aft sonar began to ping quietly.

'Looks like we've got company,' Amy said.

'The low swimmers are awake and they probably know where we are,' the Doctor said. 'It won't take long for them to figure out what we're doing.'

'Where's this tunnel entrance?' asked Rory.

'It's deep,' the Doctor said. 'About six hundred and thirty metres.'

'Don't submarines collapse if they go too far down?' asked Amy.

'The *Ocean Explorer* has a crush depth of about six hundred and fifty metres,' the captain said. 'We should be okay.'

For the next few minutes they dived in silence, with only the quiet *ping* of the sonar reminding them that they were not alone in the murky depths.

When the depth gauge read 627 metres, the Doctor pointed to something on the screen. The forward lights played on the seabed and illuminated a jagged black hole below.

'Are we really going to fit through that?' asked the captain. 'We'd better slow down so we can steer more easily.'

The Doctor and Rory pulled back on their wheels and the submarine slowed, nosing forward bit by bit into the underwater tunnel.

'Breathe in!' the Doctor joked. Amy smiled, but the other two looked very serious. She coughed and went back to checking the sonar.

'Amy, I need you to monitor the forward sonar now,' the captain said.

'We'll just have to assume we're being followed,' the Doctor added.

Amy nodded and switched the sonar controls so that the alert would sound if the submarine was too close to the edge of the cave. The sonar would also be able to map what the tunnel looked like.

'Ah . . .' said Rory. 'We might have a problem.'

On the screen, the sonar was showing a sideways-on image of the tunnel. They could all see that, instead of sloping up, the tunnel seemed to be heading down. The depth gauge read 638 metres now.

As it passed the crush depth of 650 metres, the submarine began to creak. Amy looked about nervously.

'Don't worry,' said Jane. 'When they build these things they always allow a bit of leeway on the collapse depth.' She didn't sound convinced of her own words.

'She'll hold together,' the Doctor said.

There was another menacing creak and a tiny spurt of water sprayed in Rory's face. He flapped his arms about. The Doctor dug in his pocket and pulled out a piece of modelling clay. He reached across and placed it over the small hole.

The depth reading flicked to 656 metres.

'Do you know what sardines call a submarine?'

'Oh no,' Amy said. 'Not another one of your jokes.'

'A can of people!'

Rory moaned.

'I just thought that, even if we can't raise the submarine, we might raise a smile,' the Doctor explained.

At that moment, the numbers on the depth gauge changed to 655.

'We're going back up!' Rory said. The screen showed that the tunnel was indeed rising now.

'Okay,' the Doctor nodded. 'I suggest we get a move on.'

'Very well,' Clancy said. 'Increase the speed. But, please, don't break my submarine.'

On the screen, the sonar image showed that the tunnel sloped upward, becoming steeper and steeper until it was almost like a lift shaft, pointing up vertically. As they increased speed it felt more like they were in a spaceship or aeroplane taking off than in a submarine.

As they climbed through the underground tunnels, the water flowing in the other direction became faster and faster. This meant that they had to continue to increase the speed of the submarine, but it also meant that they didn't have very much time to react to how the tunnel changed course.

By now the *Ocean Explorer* was jolting left and right, and Rory was thrown this way and that in his seat as they sped up the tunnel.

Every now and then the big metal bulk of the sub would emerge from one part of the tunnel into a new section that had air in it as well as water.

Amy looked at the water as it pounded on the navigation screens and realised that this was exactly what the Shoal had to do to reach their spawning ground. She was amazed by the strength and courage of Makron's people and she hoped they all made it out alive and as good friends.

There was a sickening crash as the submarine broke through the pouring water once more and smashed into the wall of rock beside it. A jagged piece of the cliff ripped through the front of the submarine, missing the Doctor and Rory by less than a metre. Water poured in through the gash, and the navigation screens exploded.

Then the engines faltered.

The power flickered on and off.

If they didn't make it now, they would fall back down the waterfall and into the sea far below. Through the hole in the submarine, the control room would fill with water in a moment and they would all drown.

The Doctor threw his hand down hard on the button that controlled the power levels in the engines. They were trying to switch themselves off, but he wasn't having it.

'Noooooooo!' he shouted, his face screwed up with effort.

As he kept the button pressed down with one hand, his other was pushing the square control wheel as far forward as possible – keeping the submarine at maximum speed.

Then, with a final burst of power, the *Ocean Explorer* jumped forward.

Rory glimpsed the purple sky of Hydron through the gaping hole in the sub's nose. They were in mid-air!

'GERONIMO!' the Doctor called as the sub began to fall back to the water.

The *Ocean Explorer* crashed into the side of the crater and swayed from side to side before coming to a stop at a strange angle, like a beached whale.

'So it's okay for you to say it –' Rory began to complain.

'Eggs!' the Doctor shouted and ran off through the control room, heading for the secret lab.

They all raced after him. When they got there, the Doctor grabbed two of the glass tubes and his three companions took one each.

They staggered through the twisted corridors of the submarine up to the hatch in the side of the tower.

'I'm sorry,' the Doctor said to Captain Clancy.

'What for?' she asked. 'We made it!'

'I know.' The Doctor unlocked the metal door. 'But I did break your submarine.' He kicked open the hatch and stepped out into the sunlight.

A hundred low swimmers had surrounded the crashed ship. Their forked weapons were all pointed at the Doctor.

Admiral Icktheus stepped forward and his skin pulsed angrily.

*Kill the humans!*

# Chapter 18
# Arrivals and Departures

'I don't think you want to do that, Admiral,' the Doctor replied.

Icktheus stared in horror at what the Doctor was holding. He recognised the small dark balls in the glass tubes instantly.

*Lower your weapons!* he ordered his commandos. *He has the roe!*

The soldiers did as they were told.

Rory stepped out beside the Doctor and Amy followed him, with Captain Clancy bringing up the rear.

'Now what?' Amy asked. 'We can't hold these eggs hostage.'

'We're not holding them hostage,' the Doctor said. 'We're just holding them! I'd never do anything to hurt them. Now, Admiral Icktheus on the other hand has a nasty little mind so he thinks nasty little thoughts. Without asking us, he has assumed we are doing what he would do.'

'That doesn't answer the question, Doctor.' Amy looked sideways at him.

'We just have to wait . . .'

'What?'

'For Makron and his father!'

Almost as he spoke, there was a deep, loud flapping sound. A vast flying fish the size of an aeroplane appeared above the edge of the crater, then landed in the lake. On its back were thirty or so Shoaly. Amy recognised Makron and Darkin among them.

Darkin climbed down from the flying fish and approached Icktheus. Makron ran along behind, holding the Doctor's translation device.

'Stop this, Icktheus,' Darkin said. 'These creatures are not our enemies.'

'You are soft and weak,' Icktheus replied. 'I have over one hundred troops. You have a handful. I will not surrender my advantage that easily, governor!'

'I thought you would say that,' Darkin said. At that moment, an even louder flapping sound filled the air.

It was coming from everywhere. More than fifty flying fish appeared, surrounding the top of the water volcano. Each one had thirty or so low swimmers on its back, and all of the low swimmers were wearing the belt of purple seaweed that represented the Assembly.

Icktheus bowed his head. He knew he had lost. Two of the Assembly's low swimmers stepped forward and locked the admiral's fins in what looked like silver handcuffs.

'You are under arrest for treason, admiral,' Darkin said. 'I will see to it that you have a fair trial.'

The admiral was led away on to the back of one of the flying fish. With an enormous roar from its huge wings, it lifted into the air and dived down, away from the Fount.

The Doctor handed his jar to Rory, then climbed down the submarine's external ladder. He rushed forward to greet Darkin and Makron.

'These are yours, I think,' he said, showing the high swimmers the tubes with the eggs in them.

'They can join the others,' Darkin said.

The Doctor looked at the beautiful, violet-coloured water of the lake. It was full of the dark fish eggs. He smiled. 'May we?' he asked.

'By all means.'

The Doctor waved Amy, Rory and Captain Clancy over to him. They climbed down the ladder, careful not to disturb the eggs in their protective tubes, and Amy reached the Doctor first.

'Go on, then,' the Doctor said, gesturing at the water.

Amy didn't have to be told twice. She unscrewed the lid of the jar and bent down by the water's edge. Then she gently poured the liquid into the lake. With a satisfying splash, the egg tumbled into the Fount. Rory and Jane did the same, as the Doctor added the last two.

'All safe and sound,' he said.

'Not bad for a day's work,' Rory agreed.

'We stopped a war,' Amy added.

'And returned some baby fish to their nursery,' Clancy reminded them.

'Not a nursery,' the Doctor said, looking stern.

'What?'

'Baby fish don't go to a nursery,' he said.

'No?' Captain Clancy was confused.

'Baby fish go to plaice school!'

Both Amy and Rory started hitting the Doctor's arm.

'Ow! Stop that!' he said, laughing.

'Only if you stop telling such rubbish jokes,' said Amy.

'I promise,' the Doctor said. 'Cross my hearts.'

Suddenly there was another loud whooshing sound. It wasn't the flying fish this time, but something much bigger: the *Cosmic Rover.* It glided down through the clouds and sat above the mountain, awaiting instructions like an enormous, obedient dog.

Captain Clancy took out her radio and started talking to the on-board computer.

'Ah,' the Doctor said. 'The ship. Excellent. Yes, I think we should get back, find the TARDIS and then –'

'The Tower of London?' Amy asked.

'Ha! Yes. The Tower of London.'

Captain Clancy finished talking to the ship on her radio and stepped forward. She put her head on one side, looking at the Doctor as if he was a complicated painting she was trying to work out. 'You're not really from Head Office, are you?' she asked. 'You're not really in charge of Health and Safety?'

The Doctor put his hands on hers and bowed his head to her ear. 'That depends,' he said quietly.

'On what?' she whispered back.

'Whose health and safety you're talking about!'

**The End**

# Titles in the series:

BBC
DOCTOR WHO
DEATH RIDERS
Justin Richards
It's not all fun at the Galactic Fair . . .

The Galactic Fair has arrived on the mining asteroid of Stanalan and anticipation is building around the construction of the fair's most popular attraction – the Death Ride! But there is something sinister going on behind all the fun of the fair: people are mysteriously dying in the Off-Limits tunnels. Join the Doctor, Amy and Rory as they investigate . . .

The Doctor finds himself trapped in the virtual world of Parallife. As the Doctor tries to save the inhabitants from being destroyed by a deadly virus, Amy and Rory must fight to keep his body in the real world, safe from the mysterious entity known as Legacy . . .

The Doctor, Amy and Rory are surprised to discover lumps of moon rock scattered around a farm. But things get even stranger when they find out where the moon rock is coming from – a Rock Man is turning everything he touches to stone! Can the Doctor, Amy and Rory find out what the creature wants before it's too late?

The Eleventh Doctor and his friends, Amy and Rory, join a group of explorers on a Victorian tramp steamer in the Florida Everglades. The mysterious explorers are searching for the Fountain of Youth, but neither they – nor the treasure they seek – are quite what they seem . . .

Terrible tiny creatures swarm down from the sky, intent on destroying everything on planet Xirrinda. As the colonists try to fight the alien infestation, the Eleventh Doctor searches for the ancient secret weapon of the native Ulla people. Is it enough to save the day?

A distress signal calls the TARDIS to the *Black Horizon*, a spaceship under attack from the Empire of Eternal Victory. But the robotic scavengers are the least of the Eleventh Doctor's worries. Something terrifying is waiting to trap him in space . . .

The Eleventh Doctor treats Rory to a trip to the Wild West, where the TARDIS crew find a town full of sleeping people and a gang of menacing outlaws intent on robbing the local bank. But it soon becomes clear that Amy, Rory and the Doctor are not the only visitors to Mason City, Nevada . . .

An ancient artefact awakes, trapping one of the Eleventh Doctor's companions on an archaeological dig in Egypt. The only way for the Doctor to save his friend is to travel thousands of years back in time to defeat the mysterious Water Thief . . .

People are mysteriously disappearing on Moonbase Laika. They eventually return, but with strange bite marks on their bodies and no idea where they have been. Can the Eleventh Doctor get to the bottom of what's going on?

The Eleventh Doctor and his friends head to the 1966 World Cup final. While the Doctor and Amy discover that the Time Lord isn't the only alien visiting Wembley Stadium, Rory finds himself playing a crucial role in this historic England versus West Germany football match . . .

The TARDIS crew are quarantined in Terminal 4000, where the hideous Desponds have destroyed the hopes of all waiting passengers. Can the Eleventh Doctor and his friends save the day by helping everyone to escape, without succumbing to despair themselves?

The Eleventh Doctor and his companions are on board the *Cosmic Rover*, a spaceship orbiting the water-planet Hydron. Joining the crew, they journey underwater on a scientific exploration. But nothing is as it seems on the high-tech submarine. When a virus infects the crew, the Doctor discovers the ship is hiding a dangerous secret . . .